T0365052

INTO THE NIGHT

R. A. B.

authorHOUSE®

AuthorHouse™
1663 Liberty Drive
Bloomington, IN 47403
www.authorhouse.com
Phone: 1 (800) 839-8640

Published by AuthorHouse   05/06/2015

ISBN: 978-1-5049-1029-3 (sc)
ISBN: 978-1-5049-1028-6 (e)

Library of Congress Control Number: 2015906767

Print information available on the last page.

Any people depicted in stock imagery provided by Thinkstock are models, and such images are being used for illustrative purposes only. Certain stock imagery © Thinkstock.

This book is printed on acid-free paper.

I T WAS ALWAYS THE same thing every night, she tossed and turned in the hot atmosphere of the night. Never failing, it never seemed to end. Even the ceiling fans, portable fans, any type of fan didn't seem to work for her. Her mind was on constant speed, her insomnia forever rearing its ugly head. Something she had dealt with since she had been a teen, even took medication for it, but it only made her feel like shit in the end. She was someone that no one believed in, and that was part of the problem. Or maybe that was half of it. Who knew anymore? But the heat, the heat consumed her body and soul. It was Texas summer time weather. A hundred degrees plus in the shade, even in the night air. It was suffocating. It amazed her why she even bothered moving away from the North, it truly did. *Oh yeah, my job that's why!* She thought to herself, blowing a piece of her hair out of her face. Hell even her parents warned her of the Texas heat. She looked over towards the opened window, hoping for some kind of breeze, and sighing knowing it was no use. *Why couldn't this state cool down at night? Why?!* She thought to herself as she got up, went to the bedroom window and looked out of it. The city lights twinkled before her. The ever present noise of cars zooming past in the distant could be heard from miles away. Or so it seemed anyways. An occasional honk could be heard, a screech of tires, possibly a siren or two, if you listened very carefully.

It amazed her how life beyond this window seemed to keep going on, as if nothing was happening around them. They all seemed to just drive forever on, in the middle of night as if they're in a rush. Either way it felt like her days seemed to drag on forever, especially in this god forsaken heat! She thought to herself. She loved her job, minus some of the people who tried to always get in her business, and she happened to be in a good relationship. Even if they hadn't seen each other much since being down here. But even so she didn't think long distance relationships would ever work between them, but he hadn't given her any reason to justify that just yet. At least from the many times they had face timed there hadn't been any reason.

She thought back to those last few days, before being located here to Texas. Her parents were trying so hard to calm her down. There was almost a few times where she had a panic attack, but she had controlled it. It wasn't something she liked thinking about, but at least it hadn't gotten out of control! She had never visited this state. *Ever!* But now that she was here, it seemed like the weather was always changing. At first she didn't mind it, but now. Now it felt like she could find her death here, especially with how hot it could get during the daytime. She knew better to complain, but *if she ever got out of this hellhole the first person she would go off on, would be the damn boss himself!* She thought to herself, flicking a bead of sweat off her face in the process. It amazed her how anyone could live here, it was a constant thought in her mind. Especially on the nights, like tonight, that she couldn't sleep cause of how hot and sticky she felt at the moment.

She then pressed her head against the glass window, it too seemed to burn against her already flushed skin. It was impossible to stay cool. *It's only temporary Emily, so deal with it!* She thought to herself once more, knowing it were true! She had managed to find a job, a job that required her to live in Texas for a year to learn everything that was required for what was needed, give or take some months if they needed her back sooner. The man that ran the company seemed like some hot shot ego maniac, that didn't even think twice to meet with her before said transfer took place. That had been, *at least*, three months ago. It had been mid-April, when she came here, and the months had flown by, she had reported back valuable information when needed, but of **all** the places they could've sent her to it just had to have been Texas. A never ending land of terrain, where all you could see in the distant was hills and mountains. The grass was to dry and the people acted as if they've never seen thunderstorms before! The traffic held no candle to what she went through in other places in the United States. She had only been outside of the states once or twice, but that was only for business occasions. After all, this was what she had signed up for to begin with!

It was then that she had realized, after pushing away from the window, seemingly unsticking herself from the window cause of the heat of the night that she hadn't called him. He's *going to be so mad!* She thought with a heavy heart! He had been her life line, her strong hold, through everything she had been through recently. And it had been days, days since their last chat on the phone. Not that did much good, especially when he had been so busy himself. But even she knew he would wonder why she hadn't called him in the first place. He had never initiated anything though, that was the downfall of their beautiful relationship. Sure, the sex was amazing! But when it came to other things, it had been her. Always her, to make the first move. And frankly she was tired of it!

"Emily!" Came the rough voice over the phone, once she had finally made up her mind and walked over to her dresser drawer to make the call. At first, she wasn't even sure if calling him this late, at night, would be a great idea. But in the end she had dialed his number.

"Mark." Came her short reply. It was too late for his attitude. *Hell it was fucking three in the damn morning for god's sake!* It really wasn't the time for it, even if it was one in the morning there. She wasn't going to start a fight when she was tired, hot, and had to be at work in a matter of hours. She could play hooky, but she had done that enough times already. But those had been valid excuses, at least she thought so.

"Why haven't you called you silly girl?! Must you be so stupid?" Mark exclaimed, his rough voice sounded annoyed over the phone. Of course it was *her* fault. Never his. She sighed heavily over the phone, pacing to and fro in the small bedroom of hers. The hot breeze doing nothing for her in the process, besides just making her even more

3

miserably hot, before sitting down on her bed. What she wouldn't do for a nice cool breeze right now!

"Look I forgot. I've been busy, you know how my job has been." She said as she opened up the door to her bedroom and walked into the hallway, that lead to the rest of her apartment. There was no use staying in her room when she couldn't sleep and the room felt like a heated oven on full blast. It wasn't any different once she had made it into her living room, it only seemed to get worse. *Great the thermostat must be* out*!* She thought with a scowl as she plopped herself down onto her couch, feeling herself instantly stick to it! That's what she got for having a leather couch!

"Yeah, yeah, your job, that sent you fucking three damn states away for the soul purpose of exploiting you for their own damn personal expense!" His answer stung, hurt even but he never knew the full details. And if he did, he never seemed to listen to her. Maybe it was time to move on and let him go. Maybe then that'll be one less headache gone. After all, she loved her books more than anyone else. She had gone into publishing for a reason, her job required her to do things that made her fall in love with books even more. Every day was something different. She loved being challenged, that's what came with the job. Hell she came along ways from being daddy's little girl! The thought of her dad made her smile inside, he had pushed her to better herself no matter how many dead ends she came across! The thought of him brought a small pang to her fragile heart. They hadn't talked for years it seemed like, when really it had only been months.

"Look *daddy* I don't have time to argue. I'm fucking hot as hell and your attitude is not something I do not want to hear right now, kapesh?" She said to him, using his nickname that she generally used when he frustrated her sexually and mentally. But even more so when she was really irritated. She could hear him laughing over the phone, a throaty one at that, before he growled. She groaned inwardly *knowing* exactly what his intentions were then. He wanted to have sex over the phone, something she wasn't too keen on before meeting him. Hell the thought of it made her giggle. He had changed her, but even so there was things he did. Still did as a matter of fact, that made her question why she stayed. Her family didn't even like him.

It had all started when they met through mutual friends. Friends who seemed to have distant themselves when they realized the things he did, said, or would do to her. He had put his hands on her once. Just once, and they threatened him. It didn't go well, especially when the cops almost had been called in that particular day. To make a long story short, it was them or him. And the fool she was at the time, choose Mark. She sighed inwardly knowing that they needed to end things. If only it were *that* easy! She thought, knowing at any minute of the day it was easy for them to part.

"If I was there *Emmers you'd* have my cock so far up that delicious pussy of yours *you'd* forget your own name." Mark chuckled as if he made *some* kind of joke. What that joke was she wasn't entirely sure. But then she heard a faint voice in the background. Something other than him turning to find a better spot to lay. She could sense something was amiss. But she *didn't* want to jump to any conclusions. "But seeing as *I'm not* you shouldn't worry your pretty little head over it."

She frowned, he had never once said something like that to her. The sound in the background *came* again, the movement of *something* more as well. She gulped and wiped away the sweat from her brow. *Fucking hell the heat is insane!* She thought to herself but also at the same time *knew* he *wouldn't* be faithful! Hell they haven't been together for over three fucking months, but it hurt even thinking about it. Tears came *unbidden* to her eyes, and she angrily swiped them away from her eyes. She always knew she hadn't been enough for him, regardless of how much he had been there for her in the many months previously she had always knew in her gut that she wasn't enough!

"Are you cheating on me, Mark?" Came the *question* she feared asking but it had to been asked. The heat of the night seemed to engulf her as the tears silently came down her face. The sound came again and then a grunt. Her answer was there. The grunt he made during their many sexual encounters over the past year. Then a harsh laugh came over the phone. One that scared her, even in her sleep. Another reason perhaps why she *daren't* dream, cause of how evil it sounded! But she knew it was her insomnia, it has played a major role in her life since she was teen. Now that she was in her late twenties, it only seemed to get worse. She absolutely refused to take the medication that had been prescribed to her, it only did more harm than good in her opinion.

"Finally she says something smart!" Mark bellowed over the phone. A giggle of a girl came unbidden over the phone. She knew that this was the last straw. The only straw that could be torn apart. Had she meant *nothing* to him? *Obviously* was the *answer*. But even so she hated even thinking about it.

The night seemed longer this time. More darker than usual. She clenched her teeth hard, to the point where she bit her tongue. She tasted blood, but it *didn't* matter to her at the moment. She didn't say anything, simply hung up on him. Their time was over. It was only then that she realized she knew their relationship was on that course since the time he had placed his hands on her.

She wiped the tears off her face, angrily, and *threw* the nearest thing at the wall with such force it broke. It wasn't of any value anyways. But the fact that he flat out had to be a dick about it, was what hurt the most. She got up from the couch, ignoring the incoming call from Mark and stepped outside. The evening was clear, it always was, but the air was still stifling hot!

Emily wasn't sure how long she stood there, on the balcony of her apartment, but she knew then that she had to move on. Move on from what was her life with Mark, not that it wasn't going to end happily anyways, and focus more on her job. It was practically the only thing that made her happy to begin with. If only the CEO of Bowling Books Publishing *would* just talk to her and not give her the run around. And as the sun began to rise over the east, she knew that day would be a long day.

"No sleep for the weary." She muttered under her breathe as she walked back inside of her apartment, slamming the door behind her. The wall shook a little with the force, but stopped after several seconds as if nothing had ever happened. The glass that was on the floor, from the vase she had broken glimmered from the sunshine peeking through the open blinds. She sighed, got some gloves from the cupboard in the kitchen and picked up the shards before throwing them away. She could never catch a break it seemed, ever! First Mark, then her job, it was as if her life was a running joke.

She sighed heavily, went to her bedroom to get ready for the day. And as she turned off the fans in her room, grabbed a quick bite to eat, Emily headed out the door in the July morning heat, hoping for something good to happen as she started up her car and headed towards BBP's Texas branch office, which was located on the outskirts of the DFW area; by Weatherford. She turned up the music and drove, drove with every intention of getting in touch with the boss himself, and to put Mark furthest from her mind as possible. She didn't need to dwell on that relationship, not when she had so much riding on the future of her job. Whatever that was, she hoped it ended in good news. And as placed her foot on the pedal, to her Mustang GT, she felt free. Free from everything, if only for a short brief time.

CHAPTER 2

THE ALARM WENT OFF in a blaring rapid motion, the constant echo of it seemed to go off into his ears like a loud trumpet sound. He groaned as he slammed his hand, onto the snooze button, before peaking up at the numbers that were bright blue in the darkness of the room. It was after five am, he had to be at the office by six for a meeting with the board of directors, which would take place at or around seven; just depended on how fast the others got there. He rubbed his eyes, before gently shaking the blonde hottie that he had shacked up with last night. She wasn't that great, but he hadn't had sex in months, with all the meetings and acquisitions he had to attend to, he just couldn't resist the temptation. He was, after all, a bachelor. One of the richest on the east coast, let alone New York anyways. He turned on the side light and shook her with some force. She mumbled incoherently in her sleep, but didn't wake up. Another reason why he didn't bother shacking up with anybody, at his place particularly was because they always seemed to find their own place in his bed and stayed there. The last one ended up sleeping the day away. Hell she was a good lay, but became a nuisance in the end. He sighed heavily, before getting up and didn't bother shaving. It wasn't as if he would need to, especially when his beard didn't grow super quick like some of the other guys he knew!

He took a quick shower, before getting dressed, and went to the kitchen. The house maid knew what he wanted, and had laid it out for him with a note saying she'd get the girl out before he arrived home later that day. He was thankful for her, she had become like a second mother. Which he didn't mind. She knew her limitations, knew that he was a busy man, and when he did take off from the office; which was very rare occasions, he had spent all day in his office. He was turning thirty next year, he didn't reach his status overnight and didn't plan on losing it overnight either! You had to play with the big dogs, per say to get where he was at! He grabbed his keys, before heading out of his two story condo that he lived in. Sure he was rich, but he liked the place he owned. Hell, he had mansions in Paris, Seattle, Louisiana, and Florida, when and if he ever decided to go on vacation. He was due for one, but he never could stay away without something major happening! Here in New York the condos were amazing to live in. They were rich with detail and design to begin with. He went down to the garage, got into his Lamborghini and drove down to his main publishing house! Something he admired, and loved, from the very start. It was his baby after all!

The traffic was light, but he knew once he got more in town it would pick up. The building was located near the World Trade Center building, the only one that they had built in memory of the fallen towers so many years ago. It was all but a memory, but it was a day that no one could ever forget. He didn't know anyone that worked there. He hadn't even lived in the city at the time, but when he saw the building. The building that became home to Bowling Books Publishing Inc., he was taken with it. Hell, no one thought the thirty floor building would ever have potential to thrive again. But he saw it for all its worth. He bought it, had contractors redo everything about it, and everything began to fall into place for him. In a matter of no one time he had a better home office for his people, than he had back in California. He chuckled slightly, knowing half of them had followed him here, while the rest stayed there. Either way the sight of the Hudson River in the far distance, and the small specks that were boats in the ocean made his day every single day. Even he could see the Statue of Liberty if he looked hard enough, though with the low lying clouds that were rolling in, he knew then he wouldn't be able to see much of anything once he got to the top.

He then parked his car into the space that was his, before getting out and going over to the ground elevator, but not before locking the doors, with his automated key ring, and going inside the cart. He pressed the button for the highest level, straightening his tie in the process. His dad had taught him how to do Windsor knots as a young boy, even if he had messed up at times, there was never a time where he used the clip on ones. Hell he wasn't even sure his dad owned any. He then sighed, as he gritted his teeth, as he shook the image of his father out of his head. He had left them. Left them for some whore in the dead of the night, never once explaining himself. He hadn't forgiven him. Especially when he had turned his life upside down as a teenager. He balled up his fist, before punching the metal next to him, as he tried to calm himself down. It was *his* fault that he had drove him to drink at such a young age. But even so he knew his limit. Well *now* he did anyways!

The doors opened, with a small ping, and all thought vanished of said man, as he stepped out and towards the double doors that would lead to his personal assistants and also his office. Which happened to overlook the city. A city which he loved, regardless of the many months that were left under the snow and ice. This one had been a bad one, the snow had been so bad this year that he had to work from home for a solid week. It was a big cluster fuck but they all managed. Even if it had meant catching up on manuscripts, himself, from his office at home. He pushed the door open and saw both of his ladies already at work. He knew they didn't get much sleep, just by the looks of their eyes.

"You know if I didn't like you two women, your asses would both be fired." He told them, with his arms crossed against his chest. They both scrambled to get their things together and gave him their best apologetic look. If he hadn't been their boss, and didn't have a rule of messing around with his upper staff, he give into it. But knew better than that. He knew he was a good looking guy. But there was a time to play and a time to work. And they knew better than to believe he'd give them a free pass.

"We're sorry, Sean." They both said at once, before looking at each other and even though they had said it were there voices, he could see the childish glee in their eyes, and he gritted his teeth. Did they *really* think that he was stupid enough to see what they were doing? He thought to himself. After all, they were the *only ones* that could call him by first name basis. Maybe that would stop soon, but he had a business meeting to attend to soon, and he wasn't going to play babysitter to them both.

"No fucking excuses, ladies. And if you two had the common decency you'd cover up your breasts while you're at it. We run a professional business here, not a whore shop." He told them in a stern voice, seeing them instantly deflate with whatever brave idea they were hatching up. He grabbed the notepad, with the day's work on it, and looked through it. That damn Emily girl was *still* trying to get ahold of him! He sighed inwardly knowing he needed to touch base with her soon, or she'd drive his PA's completely up the creek sooner or later. Later being not even a possibility if he was being honest. "And make a note for me to contact the Texas branch to speak with this Emily girl. I've put it off far enough!" Sean said to them both as he grabbed the pad and headed towards his office. He lightly kicked the door, letting it open slowly in front of him, and turned on the lights. He knew maintenance hated seeing his scuff marks, where he opened his door, on the wood but he paid his staff well. It wasn't a big deal.

He sat down in chair, turned on the Mac book pro; the newest and *latest* edition to the apple series and took a swig of the hot mug of coffee that had been waiting for him on his desk. He laughed silently to himself, knowing that those two had planned their little show, which had turned him on. He was a male, who wouldn't at the sight of big perky breasts in front of them? He thought to himself, as he quickly shook the thought from his mind though, he didn't need to get a hard on at work. Especially when he had a meeting with the boards soon. He ran a hand over his stubbly chin, as he clicked open a file of the girl that he hadn't met yet, but knew soon would have to; Emily Night.

Emily Night
Born: April 17th, 1986
Open rest of file/pic

He looked at the file on his computer, seeing the spunky looking woman come into view. She had bright red hair, freckles on her face, the brightest blue eyes he had ever seen, and looked like a bright young lady. Hell a 4.0 with honors was something, he thought to himself as he scrolled through the work of hers. Why did he refuse to see her again? He knew he had done that with previous staff, but that was for other reasons. Oh yes, research, or maybe he couldn't handle the fact she was a gorgeous lady, and got an instant hard on by looking at her. Yes, maybe that was it. Either way, he knew she was off limit, especially since it said she had a boyfriend. *Even so, she's bound to become single again, Sean!* He thought to himself, but immediately vanished the idea from his brain! But knew he would have to guard his hardened heart even more, when and if, he decided to let her come back to the main branch. He had dealt with enough in his life to know that he couldn't get close to anyone, especially when every time he got involved with a lady they only wanted him for one thing; his money. Even the ones he slept with, which were ever so often, he would make them sign an agreement form to make sure they don't come back to him asking for nothing.

He looked at the time on his computer, picked up his notes, and headed towards once of the conference rooms where the other board of directors were at. He noticed however, that they had set up a spread. One he completely forgotten about, but knew he'd eat some anyways. He had a high metabolism, worked out every day and jogged a few miles each day to stay in shape. He sat down in one of chairs, next to one of the younger men, whose name he couldn't remember, before setting his things down, waiting for the meeting to get started, he wondered if everyone was on board with the newest developments that had been brought to the table, from a different publishing house. As the meeting began, he listened to everyone's opinions on what had been brought to the table, especially the ones where they'd divide the smaller offices up and combine them for big events. He just hoped no one would get into a heated argument over anything, especially after the last meeting they had. Even so, he knew that eventually someone was bound to say something that would set off on one of these guys. They all had heated tempers to begin with, especially if they got together for a football game or a baseball game. *He being the worst of them all, they all knew how rowdy he got but didn't let that affect their business meetings, and if they had well they'd get an earful, from not just him but all of his colleagues as well.* He thought to himself with some irony as the meeting continued on.

It was a little after one in the afternoon when the meeting was finally over. He ran a hand through his blonde hair, it was short but enough to run his hand through, and shook some of the guy's hands before heading out of room. Nothing had been really resolved, so the dividing some of the offices into smaller ones wasn't going to happen. He didn't really think it would happen, but he listened and put his thoughts into it. Luckily the majority of the men thought it was a bad business decision, and even though it took the majority of his morning up it was okay. He walked back down the hallway that led to his office, noticing that his bodyguard was waiting for him in one of the chairs. He had given him the morning off, but that was because he had to attend a funeral the previous day before. He was a hardworking man, an ex-police man, with a black belt in karate. That's all he needed to know he was safe. Well, besides the gun that he knew that was holstered away on his side.

"Big boss." He said with a firm handshake, and a clap on the back. Both ladies were giggling like hyenas. He knew why, but didn't want to address it at the current moment.

"David." He said to his bodyguard, before walking over to the ladies and they immediately stopped giggling. He heard David bark in laughter, knowing what was going to come next. He'd have to tell him what these two had done earlier this morning. But that could wait for another time. "When you two are done getting hot and bothered by us, call the Texas branch and ask for Emily. Think you two can manage that or shall I write it out in big bold letters?" Sean asked them, sarcasm dripping all over his voice, but had an underlying warning beneath it. They both stopped immediately, as he walked inside of his office, David following close behind him.

CHAPTER 3

THE DAY SEEMED TO drag on forever, when really it was almost lunch time. Emily was tired, exhausted, and annoyed to the max. Her ex-boyfriend wouldn't stop texting her, apologizing for the way she had found out, and other excuses. She didn't even dare pick up the phone, because if she had shed blow up on him. After all they had been through, or what little they had, she thought he cared about her. *Loved her* even, which she laughed silently to herself about. Love. Such a big word for four letters. It really meant nothing but a big joke. Had she ever been in love? She thought to herself, as she grabbed a granola bar from her purse, before shaking her head at the mere thought of it. There was no such thing. Love was for fools, even her biological mother had once said that to her. Or maybe that had been from a friend. Either way, it wasn't of any importance to her anymore. She took a bite of the bar, as she looked up from the manuscript she was reading and let out a breath she had been holding.

Her phone buzzed once again, for what seemed like the umpteenth time that morning. She ran a hand through her fiery red locks, before letting out a small groan. She looked at the text message, and rolled her eyes. It was from Mark, once again. *Was he that desperate to get into her panties?* She wondered to herself, not bothering to hit the view button on her screen. It wasn't even worth looking at. She looked out of the open curtains, seeing the tiny millions of cars passing by on the highway below her, wishing just for a moment to be amongst them. She always felt free behind the wheel of the car, or a motorcycle. She needed to take her motorcycle out for a spin soon, she missed the wind in her hair. Not so much the bugs in her teeth, but she had always been one for a challenge. She had the scars to prove some of them too! She smiled at the memories, before turning back around in her chair and taking a swig of her coffee. It was the only true thing keeping her awake right now. Oh how she longed for sleep to find her! She thought to herself, yawning just ever so lightly.

She looked towards her computer screen, after hearing the ping sound. She pressed the button on the screen, indicating that an in-house memo was being forwarded to her, by the head of the office here. It was probably another manuscript that needed her undivided attention. She got about 10 of these, or more, she lost count really, a day! Some of which she wondered if Andrew was pulling her leg on or not. Especially when she had a good laugh over some. *Hell, she was easily amused, depending on what the situation was, and whom she was around with at the time.* She thought to herself as she blew a piece of hair out of her face, she was knew she needed a haircut but it could wait. But when the email finally opened up, she nearly dropped the pencil she had been holding. This was a joke, it had to be, especially with the many times he had *avoided* her many emails and phone calls. Hell those girls he called PA's (personal assistants) sounded like childish bitches over the phone in her honest opinion. She thought to herself with annoyance.

Miss Night,

The Big Boss from the main branch will contact you shortly.
Be on standby.

Thank you for everything you have done,
Andrew Long, Head of the Editorial Dept.
Texas Branch

She looked at the email a few times, before getting up from her desk and walking straight from her small cubicle to the head office that was down the hallway. She knocked on the door, crossed her arms and tapped her foot and she stared directly at Andrew himself. He looked at her with a bemused look on his face, as if he was playing dumb as to why she was here in his office.

"How may I help you Miss Night?" He asked, with a bemused voice. She knew, just by the look on his face, that he was clearly aware of why she was here. The look in his eyes clearly gave it away, making her roll her eyes in the process.

"*You* know exactly why I'm here, *Andy!*" She said using some emphasis on the word you and his nickname that she called him, when irritated with his shenanigans. It wasn't the first time he had tried playing this game on her, and she would be damned if she fell for it now. They had a short time fling, back when she first starting working at this division, but Mark didn't need to know that, especially now since it didn't even matter anymore, and crossed her arms. "Don't bullshit me. You've done it once before, and you know how *well* that ended up." Emily told him in a serious voice. She wanted to be sure if this was legit or another one of his pranks. The first time it had happened, she was so mad at him, that she showed up late to work for a solid week, purposely. The last day however, he had made her stay late and took her to his place where they went at like drunk monkeys. But that was then, this was now. And it definitely wasn't going to happen again!

"Ahhhh yes, I remember that *night* quite well, Emily! But no, I'm not bullshitting you, this came from his office itself. So today's your lucky day!" He said to her, his eyes still holding that same bemused look. She walked over to him, after closing the door; thankful that his office blinds were shut, and sat down on his desk. She knew that he didn't like when people turned his authority around, especially when it came to such small matters. Luckily for her, she knew what buttons to tick. How to tick them and when to do so.

"If I find out this was another cruel joke of yours, I'll fly my ass to New York City myself and talk to the big man himself. He maybe some hot ass stud, but he's on my shit list." She told him, jabbing her finger into his chest, as she looked him dead in the eyes. Their noses basically touching. She could tell she was getting to him, but there was no lie in his eyes. If he was lying, then he was definitely good at hiding it. She patted him on the head, like a dog; because to be honest she thought he was one, most men were anyways. Before walking out of his office without even saying another word. She loved getting underneath people's skins, it thrilled her even, but she knew when and where to draw the line at as well. And as she walked back to her cubicle, she still hoped this wasn't a scheme. She didn't like being played for a fool. There was always consequences for people who did that, and it wasn't always pretty. She did her fair share of comebacks as a teenager. Some she wasn't so proud about, but luckily for her she had never been caught. She chuckled at the memory of it all, before letting out a breathe. The air was stuffy in hair, just like it had been outside. She hated this heat. She really did.

She then turned on her mini fan, the highest level it could muster for such a small thing, before going back to the manuscript she had been reading previously before the in-house memo was emailed to her. She silently muttered under her breathe though, wishing things would go her way. Just once. That's all she asked. She worked hard to be where she was at not, had enough people in her past doubt her motives, and now. Well she wasn't going to let that happen again. She requested the New York branch for a reason, to live in a city that she loved. A city that seemed to forever stay awake, which fit her style. After all, her insomnia kicked her ass most nights anyways.

But then the phone rang. All thought vanished from her mind, her hands shook with anticipation. *Was this it? Was it the big boss himself?* She thought to herself, wondering and hoping; praying even that it'd be him. She picked up the phone with bated breath, closing her eyes, hoping this wasn't some trick and she wasn't dreaming.

"Hello, Emily Night from the Books Bowling Publishing incorporated speaking. How may I help you?" She said in a singsong voice, one she always used when at the office. Otherwise she would've just gone off on the person on the end of the line.

"Emily, its Sean Bowling. I heard you were trying to get in touch with me. What can I do for you?" Came the voice of the boss himself. He sounded amused, almost sarcastic even, as if he already knew why this call was being made. To her he sounded like a pompous asshole just trying to mock him. She gritted her teeth, to keep herself calm and collected. After months, he *finally* decided to give her a call! Months! Oh hell she was fucking livid as all get out. The heat didn't help her either. Did the air conditioning suddenly decide not to keep this place cool anymore? Or was it because she was seeing red that her adrenaline was running high? She thought in annoyed voice, before blowing some strands of hair out of her face.

"Well if it isn't the boss himself. After months of trying to fu.... reach you. You *finally* decide to call me. Cut the crap boss and let me come to New York." She told him flat out, almost slipping a cuss word out in the process but managed to catch herself in the process. She heard some movement in the background, shuffling of papers even, and then something that sounded like typing of keys on a keyboard. She would usually get irritated by something like this, but knew he was busy. Hell, he was the big boss of the whole company anyways. There was no telling how many employees he had to keep up with there, let alone in the five other smaller branches he owned. He was a big deal, not that she ever cared to admit that but still.

"I do apologize for any inconvenience you have encountered, Miss Night, but I thought that the...."

"You thought?! You thought?! Sorry for interrupting you, *sir*, but this state isn't even that great. Hot as hell, the people are idiots. And you..."

"Forgive my interruption, *Emily*. But you are a very dedicated woman. I was testing you. I'll give you by the end of this week to get to New York. That gives you three days, seeing as it is Monday. If you aren't here by Friday night, when we close down for the day, at six pm. Then you're out of the job. Goodbye, Miss Night." And with that the line was dead. She stared at the phone for several minutes, before putting it back on its cradle. Was he serious? Or was he just yanking her chain? She thought to herself, before a ping was heard from her computer.

She stood up for a second, looked around her, and noticed that people were staring at her. They must've heard her go off. Hell even Andrew was standing in the hallway, with a bemused look on his face. Pompous ass. She thought to herself, before sitting back down in her chair. The ping went off once more. She wasn't even sure if she wanted to look at her email right now, afraid there'd be a sudden change in heart. She bit her nails, before opening up her email. She however noticed the hushed sound of talking, probably wondering what in the hell had just happened.

"Get back to work, guys!" Andrew boomed out to the room, which caused her to let a small giggle. She didn't bother looking up, but she knew he was pissed and wanted order to the room at large. The silence, besides the typing of keyboards and scratching of both pencils and pens could soon be heard. It was as if you could drop a needle, and probably hear the end of it drop. She thought with some irony.

She then turned her attention back to the email icon, clicked on it, and looked at it. Was this guy seriously this contrite? She thought to herself, wondering if men all thought with their dicks instead of the actual brain they were born with? She shook her head just thinking about it.

Miss Night,

I look forward to seeing you on Friday. Remember if you don't make it, you're out of the job. No ifs, ands, or buts about it. Just be grateful I didn't fire you today. Further interruptions will not be tolerated.

Sean Bowling, CEO of Bowling Books Publishing Inc.
New York Division

She bit her tongue, but didn't say anything back. It was basically her one and only warning, which didn't warrant a reply back. She had a feeling they'd get under each other's skins a lot. Not in a sexual way, not at first, but in a whole different way entirely. She yawned once more, for what seemed like the umpteenth time that day, before getting back to work. Only a few more hours to go, and hopefully she'd be able to sleep tonight. At least she hoped so anyways! She thought tiredly as the day seemingly continued on.

She got up from her desk, after turning off the computer for the day, got her keys before walking towards the elevators. She had eventually talked to Mark, which didn't make her mood any better afterwords. She had found out he had cheated on her for months. It hurt her to the core thinking about it, but knew it was probably for the best that she had found out the way she did, and not the other way round. Like perhaps finding them in bed together. She shuddered at the thought, thankful she hadn't encountered that at all. He may live a few states away, but that was just *something* she never wanted to see. Ever. It had happened once before, and she'd be damned if that would ever happen again.

She walked over to Andrew's office, seeing him pack his stuff up, as she knocked on the door. She had grown fawn of this man, but only as a fellow colleague, nothing more than that. It had been an unspoken agreement that their fling would never happen again, not even if they were the last people on this planet. They had become friends, and she would miss him.

"See you tomorrow." She said to him, extending her hand out to him. She wasn't much of a hugger. Never had been to begin with. He chuckled, before taking her hand and shaking it, and then gave her a small pat on the head. She knew it had been for earlier today, but in her current state of mind she didn't really care.

"I'll understand if you don't come in." He said with a cheeky grin, before grabbing his briefcase off of his desk. Emily just smiled, knowing that was his way of saying goodbye; just not in so many words. She then walked out of his office, without saying another word, and towards the elevators.

She got into the cart, once they opened up, and waited for them to close to get to the bottom levels, so she could drive back to her apartment and start packing her stuff up. Her last day here, at the Texas branch, would be tomorrow, and the next day after she'd fly to NYC itself. It was a small window to get everything packed but she was up for the challenge. She was born ready for one to begin with. The doors opened once she got to the ground floor, and headed straight for her Mustang. She knew one thing she wouldn't miss this heat or the constant feeling she needed to wash off the stickiness from her body.

Once she got home to her apartment, after going through rush hour, she stripped herself of her clothes the moment she closed the door. She was so exhausted, physically and mentally. She debated taking her insomnia pills, but knew; with how tired she was feeling currently, she wouldn't need them. Turning on the ceiling fan, she climbed into bed, not bothering putting any clothes on, and went straight to dream land the moment her head hit the pillow.

CHAPTER 4

GROWLING IN FRUSTRATION HE slammed the phone down back on the cradle. He couldn't believe the nerve, the nerve, she had to interrupt him. Hell, not many people did that and got away with it. But the fact he was also turned on by the sudden outburst from that woman, was also a whole other story. He quickly typed out an email, giving her three days to be here. If she *wanted* to be here that badly, then he wasn't going to give her much leeway. None whatsoever! He thought to himself, irritated. He needed a stiff drink or to punch something one. He wasn't entirely sure what he wanted more at the moment. He looked up towards the table, which David sat at pretending to read an article of some sorts. But even he knew better than to believe that, especially when there was a smirk on the older man's face. He rolled his sleeves up just a bit, before looking back towards the computer screen. Why was he letting this girl get under his skin so bad? Why? The last time he did that, he ended up being used. He thought to himself thinking of the memory.

Hell that was the last relationship he really had. The lady wanted his money, tried to say that, in the end, that he wrote her a note saying once they were married she'd get half of his assets. Which wasn't even true. He had never asked her hand in marriage, nor did he ever think it was ever going to end in one. He ran his hand through his hair, hoping that this wasn't going to turn into another money seeking bitch! He hoped, as he heard a snicker come from the place his bodyguard was at. He gritted his teeth, already knowing what the other man was going to say.

"Can it, David. If you think for one second...."

"That she already got under your skin, that you will what? Deny it?" David said, finishing the sentence with a bark of laughter. They both knew that something was going on, what that was neither could place their finger on it.

"Me? Deny something? Never!" He said sarcastically, as he got up from his chair, and walked over to the other man. He took the paper, that he knew David hadn't truly been reading from the start, and threw it away in the trash can that was next to the small table. The only table in the room that contained various magazines or newspapers that his PA's seemed to think he'd want to read in his spare time. He never had a spare moment to even bother with them, but refused to let them know that. "Do an extensive background check on Miss Night. If anything comes up, that you think needs my attention, get back to me." Sean said in a serious tone, he wasn't going to take any chances. He had dealt with enough people in his life that tried to get to him for his money. And he be damned if this Emily girl would be the next.

"Never thought you'd ask, boss!" He told him, as he stood up and they both shook hands. A firm understanding that they both had for each other, without saying much of anything. He was like a father figure for the man, especially with all the lunatic women that seemed to lunge themselves at him. He watched as his main bodyguard walked out the door and towards his office. Which happened to be on the same level as him, but no one could enter it unless they used their handprint, from their palm or the key that was given to them. Only a select few were allowed to enter that room. Mainly him and his bodyguards; he had a total of five of them. Not all of them were needed at the moment, but they were always on high alert. Especially when there had been random fires, or unusual packages, or some crazed girl that had been drugged up on some drugs, as of late. He wasn't going to let his guard down. Not now. Not ever.

He walked over to the window, before opening up the door, which led to the balcony on this level and walked outside. He placed his hands on the rail, looking at the view before him. It was absolutely breathtaking, and to think he once was afraid of heights was something. He had overcome that fear, a very long time ago. Or so it seemed like a long time ago, when really it had only been a few years ago. The clouds were no longer blanketing the city, and he was thankful for that. The sun was basking everything in its sight with its warmth, something he was thankful for. The winter had been a long one. They always seemed to be long, but now seemed to get even longer. He wasn't sure how long he stood out here, feeling like a master of his very own empire in a town of small tiny ants below him, but he knew he needed to get back to work. It didn't stop when he did, so the short break he took was welcoming, if only for a little while.

He walked back over to his desk, just as his computer pinged reminding him of another meeting that was coming up within the hour. He loved hearing fresh ideas from other companies around the world. He wasn't very fluent in any language besides his own, but then again he was thankful for the translator that would be among them. He went back to the paperwork that he hadn't finished from earlier, and took a sip of his mocha late coffee before reviewing some of the notes that other departments, on the lower floors, had made. He still wanted to be the final say in things, it made him feel like he was apart of the company he created, even though he was the CEO of it.

The ping came again, a little later on, and as he straightened up his desk; picking up the paperwork he needed for this meeting, before getting up from his desk and headed towards the doors that led him out to the main hallway. Both his PA's looked up, as he walked out, as they talked on the phone. He waved to them, which they just smiled back at him, as he walked down and towards the left where the conference rooms were at.

The day went on, and it was near closing time for the night, when Sean finally packed his things up for the day. He had a busy afternoon, which always exhausted him but thrilled him at the same time. He shut down his laptop, placing it on the charger that was next to it, and turned the security lights on. Maintenance would be in here later to clean up whatever he had had left behind. But they knew he didn't leave much behind, he hated leaving trash anywhere. He was a clean freak, but even at home his maid refused him to clean up. He knew that she loved her job, so he tried to leave something behind for her. Even if it really bothered him.

He walked towards the doors, opened one of them up, and noticed both girls were packing up their things for the day. They could be *a bit* immature at times, but at the end of the day they got their job done, which made him extremely happy. They knew how to push his buttons, and he always pushed back. It was a battle almost to see who could go the furthest at times, but in the end their business professionalism and their friendship weren't mixed in with work.

"Have a great night, Lucy and Pam." Sean told them with a nod of his head, before following David, who had been patiently waiting for him near the elevator doors, to head out for the night. He hadn't heard from him since earlier, after that phone call with Emily. He wondered what had become of the background check, but he wasn't going to ask until they were out of ear shot of people, meaning his PA's and the staff that would eventually be in the elevator with them.

The doors opened, just as the girls joined them, giggling away about something or another. He shook his head, wondering why girls giggled over the stupidest things sometimes, and looked towards his bodyguard who seemed to have the same wonderment plastered over his face. He had never figured out what was so funny between the two of them. Nor did he want to. Once the doors had closed, they had gone to a hushed whisper. Another thing he'd never understand. Who was he going to tell their gossip to anyways? He wondered to himself, knowing it wouldn't be anyone.

"What in the hell are you two whispering and giggling about now?!" He finally asked in an annoyed tone. They both stopped what they were doing and looked at him, then at David, but never said a word. Was it that *bad* they couldn't confide in him? Sure, he was the boss of them, but it was after hours it shouldn't mean anything to him, unless it was another stupid ass rumor about him again. A month ago, there was one that was about him having anal sex with a man in his office after hours once. It was rather amusing, but when he found out who it had been, their ass had been fired on the spot. And was no longer welcomed on the property, no matter how much he begged and pleaded.

He sighed inwardly, as the girls didn't say anything, the doors pinged open for some more people to come in. It was like this the whole way down, until they all got out of the cart and towards the underground garage was at. They had to go through some double doors first, before reaching it. But once there, he went his own direction with David following behind him. The girls could still be heard, in the distance giggling about something that now he wished he knew about. Sometimes he wondered why he didn't hire a pair of men for his PA's, less hassle with them but ego was always a factor. There was no telling, when and if, they'd try to find a way to one up him. He couldn't risk that. He then stopped in his tracks, noticing his car wasn't there, but the one used regularly for safety protocol. Not that it mattered, but he wanted to feel the rev of the engine; the power at his hands once more. After all, he had a number of fast cars for that reason. The feel of the engine purring under him, while he drove, always got him hard. Not for sex, but for the immaculate power they all held.

"I had Charles take her home. I figured you'd want to discuss the BC after work was over." David told him, using the code name for the background check just in case someone was listening in on their conversation. He couldn't take any risks, none. He had slipped up once, and that was one to many. The man he had mentioned was one of the guys who he had just hired. A skinny guy, who from the looks of it was intimated from the very second they had met. It was funny thinking about it. The kid was definitely wet behind the ears, fresh out of training. But if David saw potential in someone, he wasn't going to question him. At least for now of course. He opened up the passenger side door, placed his briefcase down on the ground, waiting for the other man to start the engine of the Escalade.

"I figured you'd get back to me sooner, D, but with that new kid you hired I'm sure you had your hands full." He said to him, with a cheeky grin on his face. If only he had been down here earlier, to see the look on the young boys face; he was twenty-one if memory served him right, as he took off in his Lamborghini! He knew not everyone could handle the power of such cars! Hell at first he couldn't, but the thrill behind the wheel was something else. "To have been a fly on the wall, as the kid drove off in my car. I bet that was hilarious!" He said laughing slightly at the mere thought of it. Even if he was now worried how his car made it home in one piece or not.

"It was a rather funny sight, when I told the kid he had to drive your beauty home. Thought he was going to shit his pants honestly." David said with a bark of laughter. It almost sounded like a giant boom inside the confines of the car, but he was so used to it by now it didn't make him jump anymore. Well, when he didn't expect it he did. "As for Emily Night, she's clean. Save the rough childhood that is. Her parents divorced, when she was five. They stay in touch though, for her sake. She broke a few bones, doing dangerous stunts as a teen. Loves fast cars, from what I gather. Has a couple of motorcycles. I see nothing wrong with her, besides her love for adventure. A girl *after* your own heart I say." The man finished, almost in a sarcastic way. He shook his head, regardless if the girl sounded amazing from what he just told him, it wasn't ever likely going to transpire into anything. His rules of not dating anyone, had worked so well and he be damned if he was going to break them now! He thought inwardly to himself.

"Not happening! Just cause I love my fast cars, and love testing the limits in them, doesn't mean this girl will make me see the light. You may have seen amazing things in your life, but girls only want one thing from me; my money." He told the other man, clenching his fists in the process. He wasn't going to risk anything, for anybody. Hell, if he had to be a bachelor for the rest of his life then so be it. It wasn't hard for him to get a lady for a night of sex. He had always had that easy, but even so he used condoms. There was no telling what some of them had nowadays.

He knew David wanted to say more, could tell from the deafening silence in the car, and the scowl that had become visible on his brow, but never said anything. The usual argument always ended up with them not talking to each other; besides the usual protocol stuff, for several days. He knew not to cross the line. At *least*, not this time. He looked out the window, watching the city lights twinkle and blur pass them as they got further out of the heart of the city. The traffic however picked up some, near one of the exits that led him to where he lived. From what he could see, they were doing construction on a certain part of the road. He hated that, if it wasn't something. It always another thing with the road. He took his headphones out of his bag, put them in his phone, and as the lyrics to; *Love in this Club* by Usher started playing, he closed his eyes and let the beat of the song drown into him.

By the time they finally pulled up into the drive of his place, he was getting sitting still in his seat. He had never been one for long trips on the road, it always made his joints hurt. He was thankful for the invention of airplanes, especially when you could move about the cabin, once safely in the air. He got out of the car, grabbed his briefcase, before shutting the door, as he opened the garage door; to where his Lamborghini was at. He checked over every inch of her, making sure there was no scratches of any kid on the paint, and once he was satisfied he walked inside. The young kid was sitting at the bar, drinking a glass of wine, before sitting straight up as if he had done something wrong. He laughed at the sight, shaking his head some, before heading over to the warmer; where he knew his food would be at.

"At ease, kid. No need to panic or shit your pants. David should be in the office now, you should be in there you know." He told him, with a scowl on his face. Charles jumped up, almost knocking the glass over, before rushing off to the adjoining mini house, which was attached to his place. He shook his head, hoping his head of security knew what he had hired, because all he saw was a punk kid; who couldn't see his head from his ass if it wasn't attached to his body. He looked down at the food, noticing it was his favorite; chicken spaghetti with all the fixings to it. He really needed to give his house maid a raise, not that she didn't get one every chance he thought was necessary. It was just that she was an excellent as hell cook, or maybe he was biased. He thought to himself, but shrugged his shoulders as he devoured the food.

After placing the dishes into the sink, he grabbed his glass of wine; nothing really fancy, seeing as he wasn't in the mood for such thing, and walked towards his office. He left the door open, just out of habit. There was no telling if the guys would pop in, or his maid would drop by for the evening. He turned the TV on, for background noise. Half of the time he didn't bother listening, most of the news seemed to be bad nowadays, never good to begin with as he booted up his laptop. Just because his office was closed for the night, didn't mean his job was ever done. He opened up a few files, which he took out of his desk drawer, and dived right into what needed his attention the most.

CHAPTER 5

IT WAS STILL DARK out, by the looks of it, but that wasn't what woke Emily up, the constant pounding on the door was what done it. Or possibly, the fact that her body was stuck to the sheets once more was another reason. The fans were on high, but the heat always seemed to sneak its way around the cool breeze, it was annoying He say through hell! She thought to herself, as she sat up on the bed. She was thankful that she didn't bother wearing any clothes, her body was a fine sheet of sweat, and as she got up to head towards the bathroom to start up a shower, the knocking became louder, more persistent like it seemed. She frowned, as she took the robe off of the door, and wrapped it around her drenched sweaty body. She clenched her teeth, as she felt even worse with the robe wrapped around her. The fabric only seemed to rub against her naked flesh, to the point her skin felt raw.

Once she made sure she was presentable, she walked over to the front door, looked through the peep hole, and gasped silently. It was Mark. Why was he even here? She thought to herself, as she turned the hall light on, and opened the door up. They both starred at each other, as if they couldn't believe what was going on. She had no idea he was coming to Texas, noticing that his shirt clung to him in the heat of the night. Sweat beading down his face like rain, and his pants seemed to have shrunk in the air. She wanted to laugh, wanted to scream, or maybe jump his bones. But she was paralyzed to the spot, wondering what in the hell was going on.

"Are you going to let me in? Or shall I turn into a puddle out in this fucking heat, woman?!" He said through clenched teeth. She didn't move from the spot, but pulled the robe closer to her, realizing she was naked underneath and didn't want him trying anything. Sure, it had been months! Months since she had some rough sex, but he had *no business* being here. None at all! She wasn't sure if letting him inside was a good idea, but she knew it was rude to just let him stay out here as well. She licked her lips, before stepping aside. The part of her, which wanted him to stay in the sweltering heat and die of dehydration didn't win out. She wasn't that cruel! Not like some people in her past had been to their exes. One chick had burned her man's clothes up once, and another had keyed his car. She wasn't like them. It was better to stew, then to take revenge out on an ex in a childish way.

"Why the fuck are you here anyways?" She finally asked, after closing the door behind him. She turned the living room light on noticing it was just after four in the morning, on the clock that was on the wall. It was clear she wasn't going to go back to sleep. Once she was up, she was up. It was a blessing and a curse at the same time. Just like her insomnia happened to be as well. He moved closer to her, she stepped back, putting her hands in front of her as a signal to stop. He laughed at the gesture she made, as he took another step forward and she stepped back once again.

"Stop being childish, Em." He said in a low tone, as he pushed his way past her hands and held her. She could smell the cheap cigarette and hard liquor on his breathe. She gulped, hoping he wasn't too far gone in a stupor that he'd try to make her have sex with him. It had happened once before, but even then she had managed to stop him before anything had happened. He pressed his body against hers, and she could feel the rigid form of his erection against her body. She tried pushing him away, but he held her tighter, in a vice like grip. "We may not be together anymore, but you want this. You know you do." His breathe was foul, the smell making her sick just by the thickness of it. She pressed her hands once more onto his chest, pushing him away but it was no use. He hadn't ever done this before. It was as if he was playing some twisted game with her mind, and she hated it. Her body was bowing to the feeling of his erection against her leg, she could feel it.

"I don't want you, Mark." She said in a low whisper, as he placed one of his hands near her breast as the other one snaked its way to the sash of her bathrobe. She could play at this game, could play at his sick twisted expense, she had done this before. They had played in the bedroom before, but even so this wasn't a game. He was actually scaring her, by the look in his eyes and the stench of his breathe. He had never been one to get drunk, to the point where he'd taken advantage of her, but then again she had never really known him at all did she? He had cheated on her since the beginning, without her even realizing it. How could she when she was always reading a new book or constantly working? She thought to herself feeling the heat, as always close around her.

He moved the sash of the robe, till it unraveled and fell to the side. One of her breasts peeking through the opening. Her breathing quickened, not from being turned on, but out of fear, as he traced the outer edges of her boob, before traveling over to the other one doing the same. She looked him straight in the eyes, seeing how blood shot they were. His pupils dilated with lust, and his breathe smelled even worse this close up. She stepped forward, seeing the smirk of a smile come across his face, before she kneed him straight in the groin area. He hunched over, almost instantly, as he tried to reach for her ankles. She kicked him in the face them, blood coming out from his nose almost instantly. She knew she had broken his nose and frankly she didn't give a damn!

"You will **never** touch me again! Ever!" She screamed at him, before wrapping the dash around her once more. She felt like this was his purpose, to come to Texas to rape her. To see how weak she was, but he knew that she wasn't. Hell, she had beat people up once before, and would do worse to him, if he laid another finger on her. He knew how bad her temper could get, and he had crossed the line.

"You bitch!" He yelled out, trying to throw a punch at her, but she blocked it and hit back, seemingly punching him in the eye. She raced to her bedroom, feeling the hot air clasp around her, as she dialed nine one one to report the damn fool. She was thankful that he could hardly get up off of the ground, and within minutes the police showed up and arrested him on the spot they could see, the moment they had come up to apartment, that he was under the influence of something, what she had no clue of, and was drunk. Him cussing all the way, wishing her to go to hell and other such nonsense. Tears, unwillingly, came to her eyes as she felt gross, not just from the summer heat, but the way he had looked and smelled. She wrapped her arms tight around herself, as she shut the door to her apartment and took a shower. A very long one, to get the feeling of his touch and the stench of smell off of her! She knew it was going to be a long day. A day she knew would haunt her for many months to come.

She arrived at the office, a few hours later, wishing she could just leave the moment she had come in. The fact that she still felt him on her skin, no matter how hot she had made the water in the shower earlier, she still couldn't shake it. She was strong, yes, but even the strongest people had their weak moments at times. She sighed inwardly, noticing, as she had stepped out of the elevators, and down the hall to where her cubicle was at, that Andrews door was closed. *Must be on a conference call.* She thought to herself, with a small shrug as she continued on to her area. Once she got there, a sticky note was on her desk saying have a great last day and the usual we will all miss you at the end of it. She laughed a little before throwing it away. No one, besides Andrew, would miss her. Hell even that was kind of questionable if she really thought about it! She then opened up her laptop and got to work. She needed a place, preferably close to the New York office, and fast. She knew her way around Times Square and Broadway central, but not the apartment or condo side of things. Good thing she had money set back. She thought to herself happily, as she typed in the search engine on yahoo.

By the time noon had come around, the room was filled with talk and chatter on the phones. Andrew had come by earlier, but only for a brief second, and continued on. She knew that he was busy, after all he had a lot on his plate every second of the day. It just seemed like a lot more than usual today. She placed some of her things in the bag she had brought, which wasn't much to begin with. She liked to pack light, in case something bad happened or things didn't go according to plan. Hell, sometimes if it was 'in the moment' kind of thing, then she went for it. No reason to ask questions first, with whatever she was doing at that precise second, than ask at the beginning. Maybe that's why she almost snapped her back in half while on her motorcycle a few years back. She laughed at the memory of it, before frowning. It wasn't a very fond memory, especially when her father had come to the hospital that night and ripped her a new one. Where would she be today if that hadn't happened? She thought with a bit of irony, definitely not here, that's for sure! But she wasn't going to dwell on it for long, because at that precise time in her life she wanted to live on the edge of death, and when that happened. It was a definite eye opener, which was for sure. She still loved going fast, but also knew when to take her time as well.

She took out her brown bag, which had her lunch in it, and walked to the lounge. She had only made a sandwich and chips today. Nothing fancy, especially after the events of this morning. She closed her eyes briefly, as she sat at the table, wishing that had never happened. The police had informed her, via phone call that he had several warrants out for his arrest in California. Which was a surprise for her, seeing as she had never pictured him doing anything illegal, but that was before last night happened. She thought with a heavy sigh as she dug into her sandwich. *Why did she always pick the wrong guys?* She thought as a silent tear slipped down her face. She wiped it away, not wanting to get sentimental at work. Was there ever going to be a man who she could trust fully without the promise of heartbreak? She wondered, as she continued to eat her lunch. The lounge slowly filling up with other members of staff, the chatter slowly growing louder by the minute.

Andrew then ventured into the room, she had only noticed this when the chatter had instantly died down. She looked up towards the sink, where he stood, his arms crossed in front of him. By the looks of things he had a lot on his mind, whatever that was must've been really bugging him. Was it because of her, since she was leaving so suddenly? Or of something else. He cleared his throat, sweeping his eyes among them, and all thoughts she had currently vanished.

"I don't have much to say, but...." He paused briefly, running a hand through his hair, and she knew instantly that something had happened. Whatever that was, didn't seem to be good at all. "One of ours is leaving today. Over to the New York main branch. She's in this very room, and even though it was last minute. We had to find her replacement." She knew when he paused that he was talking about her, he even looked in her direction as well. He smiled lightly, giving a brief nod in her general direction, but said nothing more. "With further ado, let me...." She tuned his voice out, as she noticed several people get up. They weren't thrilled with the news, but they would have to deal with it. She licked her lips, before getting up herself and throwing away her trash. She wasn't like some of these assholes who left their trash behind, like it was their home. It was gross and disgusting how some people acted as if they had to treat this place like their home. Hell, she was glad she didn't live with them.

After lunch was over, she knew it was time to leave. Leave away from this place, especially with her replacement already being there. It didn't take long before everything she had, which wasn't much to begin with, was packed up and ready to go. She had found a place, near Broadway Street in New York and glad they had something in such quick time. It was already ready, just waiting for her to move in. She had briefly talked to the manager of the place, over the phone, and was good on that end. Taking a deep breathe, she headed towards Andrews office, and gave him a quick hug before leaving the building.

The rest of the day was spent packing her things, in her apartment. The heat not making it enjoyable at all. She had tried putting her short red fiery hair up, but that had been a lost cause. The police had come by for a brief statement, but that had been all. The sun was beginning to set, when she had finally finished packing everything in boxes. She would have to get rid of the furniture and buy brand new things. It didn't bother her, seeing as the only things that really mattered was in the boxes, which hadn't been much. Her books, which she didn't realize how many she had until now, was in three separate boxes. She would have to mail everything to her new place.

There was absolutely no way she was going to pay a hefty airplane bag fee for all this! She thought with a groan, just thinking about it.

As the door to the apartment closed behind her, she walked over to the closed office; seeing as it was after hours by now, and placed the envelope that held her key in it, into the slot before going towards her car. She wiped the sweat off of her brow, thankful as all get out that she would be leaving this god forsaken state. She still wondered, as she started up the engine to her Mustang Gt, how anyone loved living here. But then another thought came to her, as she looked at all the boxes in the passenger seat and then the backseat, instead of taking a plane she would just drive all the way there. No stopping, unless it for eating or needing to use the bathroom. She had done it once before, and frankly she hated airplanes. Even with her hot streak with cars and motorcycles, she couldn't stand them. At all. She revved up her engine, backed out of the spot, before taking off into the dying light of the day. Only good thing about her insomnia, was being able to stay up no matter how much she was tired. This was going to be a long trip, as she turned up the radio and got onto the highway to speed off into the night.

It took her a little over a day, but she had managed to get to the New York State line by Thursday noon. She was tired, but she didn't wanted to waste any time and made it a straight trip, minus the mini breaks she had given herself. She drove to the apartment building, glad it was during the day and not at night, and got her key from the manager of the place. Heading up to her room, via the stairs, she opened it up to see nothing but open space. She laughed lightly at the thought, knowing that she shouldn't have expected anything to be here anyways. Thankfully there was tons of shops on and around Broadway Avenue and Times Square that she was sure she'd be able to find a bed, within an ample amount of time. It took a matter of no time to get all her boxes into the apartment, and walked out onto the balcony, smiling at the view before her!

"Beautiful." She sighed happily, feeling immensely better and not like a scorched oven as she had been back in Texas. She just hoped that *Sean Bowling* was ready for her. Hell he could be one ugly mother fucker for all she knew, and it wouldn't phase her at all. Sure, she had seen his pictures, but anyone could Photoshop or edit anything nowadays. Technology was a blessing and a curse for this generation. Sometimes, she wished they could go back in time, in the era of the fifties or forties. They didn't have much to work with, but at the same time had everything! Her grandparents had told her stories of those days, and even though the time machine wasn't invented yet, it always intrigued her to go back. Back to where everything had started. If only that were possible. She thought with a sigh, as she leaned against the railing, watching the tiny figures of people walking to and fro with no care in the world.

She walked back inside, and decided to buy her a bed and a few other essential items that were needed for her new place. Her only two wishes, as she headed out of the apartment door was; that the whole thing with Mark was behind her, even though it probably never was going to be, and that she'd make a good first impression with the CEO of this company tomorrow. As she headed downstairs, towards the busy streets of New York, she was becoming nervous. Nervous to actually live in a city she loved since she was a little girl and nervous for what would happen the next day.

CHAPTER 6

THE ALARM ONCE AGAIN seemed to blare loudly interrupting his dreams, dreams that seemed to be misguided and not so clear to him. The days had passed by in a blur of commotion, meetings with various companies seemingly taking up his days like nobody's business, but he loved it. Loved the fact it kept him going, no matter what kind of bullshit he had to deal with on the lower levels. He had to fire a few people, ones that he had been watching for weeks and were told numerous times to be on time, or else they'd be fired. That happened just yesterday, he was serious about being on time. He ran a business, a business he didn't want any errors in, and if someone was late then it'd throw the whole team off. He slammed his hand down on the snooze button, as it kept going off steadily getting louder by the second. He groaned out loud, as he turned over, looking at the clock. It was the same time as always, after five in the morning. He ran a hand through his hair, as his other found its way down his body. His dick was hard, nothing unusual, but he needed to relieve some of the pressure, before he could go to the bathroom.

He closed his eyes, as he grasped the head, stroking slowly at first, before going faster. He set a rhythm for himself, removing the blanket away with his free hand, and thought of a women riding on top of him, her breasts bouncing with each motion. It didn't take long as he felt the hot liquid spurt out onto his hand, as he grunted. He didn't really moan, unless it was during sex, but even so he let his body do the talking during such activities than anything else. He then reached over, as the last drop of his cum hit his abdomen, and grabbed the rag from the nightstand. He always kept one there just in case he had to stroke one out in the morning, as he wiped himself off. He turned the light on, from the nightstand, before getting up and going to the bathroom to shower. He wasn't one for leaving the residue stay on him all day long. It bothered him when he did, even though there had been a time or two where he had run so late for work, he had no choice but to throw on a suit and go. That didn't happen often, which he was thankful for, as he started up the shower, waiting for it to get hot, before stepping inside. The hotter the shower, the more he felt like he was actually being cleaned, even if it did scald him a bit.

Once he was done with the shower, he went to his closet to pick out a suit for the day. He saw the black traveler tailored fit with two buttons with a fit black trouser; one of his favorite suits, and took it off of the hanger. After putting it on, he made sure the Windsor knot was perfect before going out into the main hallway. David was standing near the entrance, talking to the kid. He didn't really like him, but he was growing on him. The only trouble he really had with him, was where to put him. He smirked as he saw the older man shake his head, obviously with annoyance, as he went over to the breakfast bar. His house maid, Mrs. Long, was making breakfast for them all. They always started their day early, besides the weekends; well him not so much just in case something or someone from the office needed him.

"Mr. Bowling, your breakfast will be ready soon. Would you like your usual, orange juice or coffee?" She asked with a polite smile. Even though he had told her in the past not to always be so polite with him, especially with how early in the day it was, but she would always politely smile and shake her head. There was no use, she had grown up being respectful and mindful of others. A true treasure she was, one he wondered how he got so lucky to have as a maid. She lived in her own home, which was next door to his, and worked her ass off no matter how late or how early it was. That was the only thing, when he had hired her, was that she wanted to live by herself. He had respected that.

"Orange juice." He replied, looking back at the two men who seemed to be arguing with each other. He shook his head at the sight, knowing it was too early in the morning for all this nonsense, and frankly he wasn't going to have any of it. "If you two don't act like *adults*, then I'll treat you like kids and separate you both so fast you think you just finished having sex! It's too early for such nonsense!" He bellowed at them, making both men jump at the sound. He could hear the silent chuckle, come from Mrs. Long, and he gave her a wink but didn't say nothing else. Both guys sat down on either side of the bar, making him roll his eyes. *Oh this will be a fucking ass long day!* He thought to himself, already feeling a migraine coming on. *Yep, a long ass day indeed.* He sighed inwardly, as he looked down at the plate of food that was just set down before him.

He dug in, without even saying a word to the both of them, savoring the taste of sausage and eggs into his mouth. He ate in record time, making sure he didn't mess up his suit, before getting up. He placed the plate and glass into the sink, before leaving the room. His security had long finished their coffee, and had gone their separate ways, as he stepped outside. David opened up the backseat door, the moment he was in view, before getting in still not saying a word. His head of security should know better than to act like a damned teenager, with a teenager himself. Yet, he knew Charles wasn't one, but acted like one from the get go. He watched the man start the engine up, before driving out onto the open street, towards the city.

"You think Miss Night will be here today?" David asked looking through the rear view mirror towards him. He had actually forgotten about that girl, especially with all the meetings he had these past several days over important matters. He rubbed his eyes, getting the sleep out of them, as he laughed at the question. Why? He wasn't really sure why he thought it was funny, maybe the fact he had forgotten or the fact he didn't feel like he had gotten much sleep last night. After all, the last meeting he had yesterday ran late and they all went for drinks after it had been over. He didn't stay that late, but he could feel the effects of it right now.

"I actually forgotten all about that, David." He sighed, still feeling the headache he had not too long ago, coming back. He was thankful for whomever invented Tylenol all those years ago but even that didn't always seem to help his headaches at times. He rubbed his temple, as he looked out the window, watching the lights move past them. "I just hope she's not a snob, because the way she sounded on the phone the other day...." He stopped mid-sentence, getting angry just at the thought of it. If she had been anyone else, he would've fired them on the spot. But her voice had done something to him, what that was he couldn't really place his finger on it at the moment, it just got to him. Even so, he wasn't going to let anything happen between them, he had rules. Rules that every person, that was in a management position below him, had to follow as well or they'd be fired on the spot. No romance with their superiors, no excuses either. It was the rule, and even though people had tried with their might to make up stuff in the past, as to why they didn't *technically* break the rule, if they had just gone out once. It didn't matter to him, they had still been fired regardless.

"Well, I would say go easy on her but.... We all know you won't." David said with a smirk on his face, as the traffic started pick up once they had gotten closer to heart of New York City. He had shook his head, knowing full well the only ones he had let slip past his fingers in the past, were usually the ones that used him. Not just for his money, but for lies and to cheat their way into getting what they wanted. The second time that had happened, he almost wanted to kill the person, but with his awesome lawyer he had hired things had gone his way. And everything that man had tried to take away from him, well.... It was no longer a stronghold for them. He had ruined them, like they tried him, but only because he wasn't the only one who knew about the scams the person had done.

Thinking about that time, just pissed him off, and he didn't necessarily want to be reminded of how he could've easily lost what he had grown to love. What he would love right now was for bourbon or jack with coke, he thought to himself as he closed his eyes briefly. He just hoped this day wouldn't be shitty, because by the way it was going so far it sure did seem like it was heading in that direction. He opened his eyes up, the moment he felt the vehicle go into a complete stop. They were only a few blocks from his building, and the traffic was horrible. From what he could tell there was a traffic jam, involving a cab and a bus. He growled in frustration, unbuckled his seatbelt, opened up the door; ignoring David's calls for him to get back into the vehicle as he walked the rest of the way. He knew it wasn't the best idea he had, but it wasn't the first time he had done this, but frankly he didn't give a damn. He heard the profanities, the honking, and the yelling behind him as he stopped to take a breather, before opening the door to his building.

One of the security guys handed him a water, which he thanked him for, as he headed towards the elevators. The headache coming back with more force now. He gritted his teeth, as the doors open and he slipped inside as he waited for the doors to close. He opened the water up, downing it in one gulp, feeling the cold liquid rush down his throat as he briefly closed his eyes. The doors opened, a few minutes later, stepping out he noticed both women were already hard at work. He was thankful that they were dressed more appropriately than they had been a few days previously.

"Anything that needs my immediate attention should be placed on priority number one today, girls. Secondly, anything that you don't think needs my attention trash it. I don't have time for bullshit today." He told them both, before walking off without saying another word. He didn't do this very often, but the way he was feeling right now he could rip someone a new asshole and wouldn't even care. He opened the doors to office, turned on the lights, as he walked to his desk. It was then that he realized that he left everything, including his cell phone back in the vehicle with David. "Fuck!" He yelled out, slamming his hand onto the desk after he had said the word allowed. This truly was going to be a long ass day, he thought to himself as he plopped himself down in his chair, holding his head into his hands. The headache was slowly turning into a full blown migraine and it wasn't even seven in the morning yet. He groaned wishing he had never gotten out of bed this morning, as he ran a hand through his hair, messing it up a bit. He just hoped he had made the right decision in letting Emily finally get what she wanted, only time would tell though.

The office door opened, a few minutes later, and he looked back noticing that David was bringing him his things he had left back in the vehicle. They didn't exchange words, none were really necessary at the time, as he set his briefcase down on the desk. They nodded each other and the other man walked out. He opened up the bag, got his laptop out, before sitting down as he booted it up. The sun was beginning to rise, as it began to peak through the window, it was a little after seven. He wondered when she would show up today, if at all. He had meant what he said at the beginning of the week. If she hadn't shown up before the end of the day, she would be fired. No butts about it! He licked his lips, before turning his chair around seeing that it was a cloudless sky before him. He had always loved the sunrise, it always displayed the true colors of the night sky, the same when it set. He had bought a telescope a few months back to gaze at the stars at night. Just cause he was a CEO of a publishing company, didn't mean he couldn't have fun in his down time. He laughed at the thought, seeing as most thought all he did was keep his head in the game and nothing more. Oh how wrong *those* particular people were.

He got up from his chair, walked out towards the balcony, ignoring the phone call he was getting on his personal phone. It was from one of the girls, he didn't have much interest in, but whenever they were in town they would get together and hook up. Now wasn't the time, as he looked out at the city before him. The sounds of horns from vehicles, the steady hum of repair work, and the chirping of birds could be heard every which direction. It was another busy day, like it always was no matter what time of day it was. The sound of a small cough was what caught his attention though.

"What?" He snapped at his PA, Lucy, almost instantly regretting but didn't show the emotion on his face. He wasn't always so short with either one of the, but the way his morning was going currently he wasn't in the mood for anyone's nonsense. Hell, he was in the mood to fire everyone and replace them with new people if that's what it took to make his day better. But even he knew that would just make the day even shittier and wasn't even necessary.

"Your coffee is on your desk, sir. And Mr. Hammond on the tenth floor said that a few of his artists haven't been showing up till late in the day. Want me to give him the go ahead to have him fire them?"

She asked him in a small voice, he knew she could tell he was in a mood today so she was more shy than normal. He sighed inwardly, knowing that man was scared of his own shadow, or so it seemed to him he was. He ran a hand through his hair, messing it up a bit more. He was going to need a stiff hard drink by the end of this day, he already could tell.

"Tell that man to grow a pair a balls and just fire the damn people, hell he should've done it the second day they decided not to come in on time. Shit, that man will get demoted or canned one if he keeps up this nonsense." He said through gritted teeth, before walking past Lucy, and towards where his coffee was. He took a sip, before looking at the lady before him. He sighed, knowing she hadn't ever seen this side of him like the other had. "Look I don't mean to snap, it's been a shitty day from the moment I got up this morning. Just tell that man to light a firecracker under his ass and grow some balls. If he wants me to fire people, I will, but he will be gone as well. Tell him that. Now, if that is all I would like you to have a good day." He simply said to her, dismissing her with a nod towards the door, she smiled lightly at him before leaving, he chuckled lightly as he noticed she had walked faster than usual. It was obvious he had scared her, intimated her even, which was fine with him.

A few hours had passed by, with things getting slightly better, but as he looked at the clock he noticed it was just after eleven. He clicked his tongue, wondering if Emily was ever going to show up today. He had never given her a precise time to be here, but even so he knew better than to show up at the very last minute of the day. He *hoped* that wasn't what she going go to do! He thought to himself, as he loosened his tie up a bit, as he finished typing something up to one of the board members. He had received an email a while ago about one of the clients, that Jezebel had hired on a few months back, was now on the best sellers list. He was immensely happy about that, even cheered loudly, which caused both PA's and his security to run in here thinking something bad had happened, it was a rather amusing moment. He had laughed at all their expressions, even harder when they all call him an asshole for worrying them. He shrugged at the thought of it, before he was interrupted with a beep from his inter house phone. He pressed it.

"Yes, *Pammy.*" He said with a cheeky smirk on his face, even though he knew she couldn't see it. But he knew she was rolling her eyes outside by the nickname he had given her.

"David just called up here, saying Miss Night is on her way up." Came the simple reply back, before the line went dead. He starred at the phone, then towards his office doors, wondering if this was pay back for what had happened a while ago. He just shrugged his shoulders, not wanting to believe any of them, as he went back to the work on the papers he had in front of him. But even so, he placed his pen down on the paper, steeling his fingers together wondering. Wondering if this was truth or just a prank of theirs. It would be the *first* time and he knew it wouldn't be the last time either. Sometimes, he hated waiting. This being one of those times.

The minutes past however, at least a half hour, before he growled with frustration. He knew better than to believe everything he was told. Especially when it came from the people outside of his door. But even so he could hear commotion outside of said door. Commotion that sounded like another voice, a girly one. He knew Pam's voice and Lucy's, this one was different. Younger, but not so young in way, kind of voice. It almost sounded heavenly to him, he frowned at the thought. He wasn't going to fall for someone's voice, let alone body. All the girls he had ever met wanted was his money. He shook his head at the thought of it, before straightening up in his chair, as a knock was sounded. *This is it.* He thought to himself, as the door opened up revealing both of his PA's behind *her.* The sight of fiery red hair, the brightest blue eyes he had ever seen, and a haircut that was in a bob was what caught his eyes first. She was wearing a simple black dress, cut to the knee, with high heels to match. He gulped, losing all sense of thought, as another seemed to stand at attention, which happened to be his dick. He readjusted himself, without any of them really noticing. This had already been a long day and now this was happening. Couldn't she have waited till the sun had set? He thought even though he was happy she hadn't.

She is going to be the death of me. He thought to himself, calming down his raging hormones, as he stood up to greet the woman. His PA's silently closing the door behind them. All thought escaping him, as he got nearer to her. The scent of her perfume, invading his senses, and all he wanted to do was fuck her senseless, but he had to stay professional. He had made the rule, the rule, the rule. He silently chanted to himself, as he raised his hand up to greet her.

"Sean Bowling, of Bowling Books Publishing, Inc. it's a pleasure to meet you finally, Miss Night." Sean told her, in a professional voice, even though deep inside this woman was doing something to him. Something he had never felt in his life, and instantly shut it down. He was turned on enough as it was. The silent mantra playing over and over in his head the entire time. Rules were meant to be broken at times, but that thought was immediately shot down. He had to be professional, not set himself up for disaster. He thought to himself, knowing that the rule was good. It had been for years now.

CHAPTER 7

SUNSHINE WAS ALL THAT she could see as she opened up her eyes. She groaned inwardly, feeling to warm. Feeling too cozy in her nice warm bed, but knew it was time to get up. She shut her eyes tightly, the sun blinding her it felt like, before sitting up. Today was the day. She thought to herself, with a groan. Was this guy nice or an arrogant son of a bitch, like he had been on the phone? Was he balding at the hairline, or fat? Was that the reason he was single? She thought to herself, before shutting her brain off. It wasn't of any use. Getting up though, she wondered what the time was. It wasn't central time anymore, and the coolness of the apartment felt good on her naked skin. She loved sleeping in the nude. Who didn't? She thought, before shrugging her shoulders. The only time she wore pajamas to bed was if she was visiting family, and even that was few and far between.

Her feet padded beneath her, as she looked at the clock that was on the wall. It was just after nine in the morning. But just to make sure, she checked her phone. They both said the same thing. Sighing with relief, she went over to the refrigerator to pull out the egg carton. She usually didn't have time to make breakfast in the mornings, but since she didn't have a designated time on when to be there today, besides before closing, she had decided to take her time. Or as much time as she would allow herself anyways. She got the utensils out for the eggs before doing what needed to be done to get them scrambled. She wanted to make an omelet, but that could wait for another time, as she swirled around the eggs to make them fluffy and scrambled. She turned the burner off, grabbed a paper plate and two pieces of bread. She really didn't feel like dirtying up anymore dishes than necessary and placed the eggs inside of them, before squishing it down a bit.

"Yum." She smiled happily, as she dug into her egg sandwich. There was nothing like it! She turned the radio on to one of the local stations and an old song from Britney Spears started playing; *Hit me baby one more Time*. She chuckled at the irony of the song, seeing as it meant nothing of hitting anyone. The singer had been a badass in her primitive years, now not so much. Sure, she loved her music but not of who she became today. It was sad how most singers, she grew up listening to, had wasted away. Wasted away to nothing, because of two things; drugs and fame. She sighed at the thought of it, as she took the last bite her egg sandwich, making sure she didn't get any crumbs anywhere. Throwing away the plate, she placed the pan and bowl in the dishwater before getting into the shower.

The fact that she didn't feel sticky and burning with the heat of the summer, like she had every morning in Texas, was a great feeling to her. She felt better and not like a running faucet of sweat either, it was the best feeling to wake up to! The atmosphere was different this far north, the way she remembered it as a child, when they took road trips up here to see the Statue of Liberty and all the other sites. The only thing different was you couldn't see the twin towers anymore. She thought sadly, as she squirted the shampoo in her hand, as the water sprayed its hot mist onto her backside, before rubbing in the liquid content into her hair, massaging her scalp as she did so. Nothing like the ladies at the hair salon, which she was always envious about, but as best as she could of course. She stepped back, letting it wash out of hair and go down her back. She then got the back scrubber, with the pouf on it, as she squirted the body wash on it and set to clean herself off. She didn't want to be reminded of the hot summer heat from Texas anymore, or the reminder that he had been *so close* to having his way with her. She could still feel his grimy hands, the smell of cigarette smoke, and God knows what else on his person. It was getting easier, somewhat to forget it. But even she knew he'd come back to find her. To finish what he had started.

She just hoped it wasn't anytime soon! She thought before quickly vanishing the way her thoughts were going, as she continued to use the scrubber on her back.

Once she was done, she dried off with the towel, before going towards her room and opening up the walk-in closet. It was spacious, lively, but had more room to put clothes and shoes in. She'd have to go clothes shopping soon, but now wasn't the time! She thought, as she looked at the few select work dresses she owned. Mostly black, with a few gray pencil cut ones in the mix. But she picked out the simple black dress, no plunging neck line, and stopped at the knee caps. It was classy enough for work, nothing trashy. That was something she hated about most women. Always trying to impress by flashing out what they were born with, when they weren't even cute or hot. Hell, just last week she saw a girl who wore booty shorts and acted like she owned the place. It was disturbing, and frankly gross. It was amazing how some men, well boys went for such things.

"A man would love a woman who dresses with class. A boy only wants trash." She muttered aloud. As she slipped on the dress, zipping up the back as far as it would go. It was sometimes a great thing about being double jointed. *Sometimes.* She thought with a shake of her head, before picking the heels that matched this particular dress. Nothing fancy, just something that was modest enough for work, as she walked over to the bathroom to look at herself in the mirror. Butterflies were forming in the pit of her stomach, as she brushed her red locks. She was nervous! Hell this was the man who started it all! She thought, before taking a deep breath and letting it out. It was going to be okay. Everything was going to be better now that she was here in the big apple. Or so she hoped it would be anyways.

She walked over to the window, which overlooked the city, with a smile on her face. The building that she was supposed to go to, was a few blocks over. The only reason you could tell because it was the next tallest building, seeing as the first was the rebuilt trade center. It was a beautiful building, despite what had happened all those years ago. Sure, it was over ten years ago but still it was an event that no one would forget. Unless, perhaps you were born the years after it had happened. She looked down, at the streets below her, seeing the tiny specks of people walking around. The taxis, cars, buses all driving around amongst them. She took another deep breathe, before walking over to where her purse was on the vanity and looked around the room making sure she had everything. Bed made, check, closet door closed, and check. She knew she was stalling, but couldn't help it. This was the day that she met the boss!

"Here goes nothing." She said to herself, as she brushed her hair once more, spraying some perfume on her person, before grabbing her keys as she headed out the door. But not before doing another check to make sure everything was where she had it. Not that it was much, but that would change once she had the chance to go shopping. She knew, as she walked down the hall toward the elevators, that she wouldn't normally check things over and over again, but it was the nerves. The nerves to not make a fool of herself, and nerves because she was *finally* meeting the big boss!

The doors opened up, she stepped inside, before the doors immediately closed. It was as if they *knew* that this was a big day for her. Not that inanimate things had feelings or a conscious but sometimes she thought they did. Either way, she just hoped that this man wouldn't be some hot shot jackass. She's dealt with enough of those kind of managers, and people to last her a lifetime. The doors opened, a few minutes later, on the ground floor, and she stepped out of it before going out the doors at the entrance. It would be useless to take her mustang a few blocks to the north, but she'd be damned if she walked in these heels all the way there. She was thankful for the taxi that was currently in idle, waiting for passengers to get into the back.

"Where to miss?" He asked in a thick accent. It sounded from somewhere in the Middle East, and from the name he most likely was. A turban on his head, a handlebar looking mustache with a full looking beard. It was another dead giveaway that he most likely was from that area.

"Bowling Books Publishing, Inc." was her short reply, as he said something in another language, before driving off. She looked out the window, at the hustle and bustle of the people going to the stores along the way. A few kids crying, as they came out a particular store. They obviously didn't get what they wanted. She thought to herself, as the taxi stopped in the traffic. Heavy for it being almost eleven in the morning, but it was almost lunch time so it was to be expected. A honk was heard from the side, as the car in front of them wouldn't move once the traffic started moving away. She chuckled, oh how she loved the city. It was so much more lively and active than Texas had ever been. That state was a buzzkill of boredom it seemed like to her.

A few more streets went by before the taxi finally arrived to its destination. She paid the cab driver a twenty, before stepping out of the car. Smoothing her dress out, after closing the door, she took a deep breath and looked at the building before her. The center door was a revolving, as there was two doors on either side that you could open if you didn't want to go through them. She clicked her tongue, as she walked towards the revolving door and pushed herself around before finding herself inside. A security check point was immediately to the right, and a hallway was on her left that indicated the bathrooms were down that way. She blew a piece of her hair out of her face, as she walked over to the security guy. A young skinny man, with a buzz cut and glasses stood there, almost bored looking. To her he didn't seem a day over seventeen, but even for such an empire that Bowling had built from the ground up, wouldn't hire school children. She giggled lightly before faking a cough. The moment she stood in front him, a smile was plastered on his face. A fake one it seemed like to her. She wasn't one for snitching on others, but this kid didn't seem to be very professional at all. She sighed with annoyance, already second guessing her move here, but couldn't fault one person out of the whole building.

"May I take your name, miss?" He asked, his voice sounded deep. Nothing of what a teenage school kid would sound like. Most hadn't even reached puberty, and even if they had done so they acted like they had no control of their own dicks. She cringed at the thought, but she knew it to be true. She was once a teenager herself. She immediately banished the thought out of her mind, before giving the man a smile, fixing his crooked tie in the process. He gulped, as he looked down, blushing a bright shade of red, making her laugh fully and heartedly. The door, behind the kid opened up revealing another man. One that seemed more professional than the other.

"Charles, you must not read the damned files. Sorry miss." He apologized as he looked at her briefly, then back at the other man. "Big boss said she, the one standing in front of us, would be here. I've read her file, steadied her picture." She heard him mutter something low and incoherently, but obviously to the point where the younger man slouched in his seat. She *almost* felt bad for him. Almost! "Ma'am, here is your clearance to get through. I'll call Mr. Bowling's PA's to tell him you're on the way up." He said to her, looking her straight in the eyes. She smiled, instantly liking this man, before taking the key card from him. He seemed like a big brother she could trust, and even though she knew she wouldn't get to talk to him much. She already trusted him, and that was saying something.

"Thanks." She simply said, as she headed towards the door that would ultimately lead her to the rest of the building. She was thankful for the security room, because in a big city like this you'd never know what kind of danger you'd end up facing! Her heels clicked on the marble tile floor, passing among others who were getting to their destination. It was open and spacious. A large chandelier was hanging in the middle of the room, followed by smaller ones. It was beautiful! She thought with a big smile. The entire ground floor looked like something you'd see back in the twenties or thirties. This guy must know his history. She mused silently to herself, as she headed towards the elevators, where there was tons of other people waiting in the foyer. There was eight elevators, all of which were surrounded by marble tile. She was falling more in love with this building by the second.

The elevator doors opened, one by one, as people got off and others got one. She waited till the very last one had descended down before getting on to it. A few others got on with her, chatting animatedly about the latest project they were working on. A few gossiping about something that had happened a few weeks previously. She rolled her eyes, listening to the two chatty females, before one got off one floor and several floors later the other got off. She was the last one on, after a few more stops to other floors, and the nerves had come back. The butterflies that had vanished previously, we're back with a vengeance! Her only hope was he didn't change his mind, and send her back packing. The thought alone made her want to punch the snot out of him. However, as the movement stopped and the doors slowly opened, all thought and reason vanished from her mind. This was actually going to happen. She gulped, before stepping out and watched as the doors closed behind her. She walked down the hall, her heels clicking against the floor, as she made it over to the desk of where the PA's sat. One talking on the phone, the other writing something down on the notepad.

She cleared her throat, catching the attention of both. "Hi, I'm here to see Mr. Bowling." She said simply, as both of them looked at her then at each other. It confused her a bit as to why they did that, before they both got on their feet. Maybe to make a good first impression? But why? She thought curiously.

"He's inside, waiting for you." Said the girl on her left. Her name tag said Lucy, seemed a bit spunky for her own good by the looks of it. She had wondered what these two looked like in person. Yep, definitely snobby like she imagined. She didn't say anything though, as they both led her down to his office. The other knocked, before opening up the door to the big boss's office. She rolled her eyes at the both of them, before she walked inside, immediately stopping in her tracks as she had done so. A man, a well-built man stood before her. Sandy blonde hair, cut to his ears, kind of messed up, with hazel eyes to match the gorgeous body of him. She bit the inside of her cheek, as she was instantly turned on by the sight of him. This was her boss? This hunk of a man was Mr. CEO of a publishing company? She wondered to herself, as she looked him up and down. Her thoughts steadily going southward with want and desire. Something she knew would only stay that way.

She however groaned inwardly, noticing that she was wet between her thighs not long after. She wanted to touch herself, but couldn't and wouldn't. This man was surely going to be the death of her. She didn't even notice the door had closed, till she had heard the click of the door shut behind them. They were alone now.

"Sean Bowling, of Bowling Books Publishing, Inc. it's a pleasure to meet you finally, Miss Night." He said to her, with his hand out to her to introduce himself formally to her. She cocked her head to the side, before taking it and shaking it. The electricity that sparked between their joined hands was what shocked her. It was like an instant connection to her heart and to her vagina. She gulped, noticing he didn't seem affected and it instantly threw a damper in her mood. She was reading too much into this. She knew she was.

"Emily Night." She said with a smile on her face, as he motioned for her to sit down in the seat that was placed in front of his desk. She smoothed her dress out, before sitting down, crossing her ankles at the bottom. His office was manly, fit for the stature of him. Not dull and boring like some big shot managers she had come across in the day. "It fits you." She said allowed, looking around the room, then back at the man before her. His hazel eyes staring right at her, with his head cocked to the side. An amused smile playing on his face, as he placed some papers on the desk, pushing them before her.

"These are what you need to know about your job. It's more in detail, than it was in Texas. You have the option of starting today, or waiting till Monday. Andrew sent me an email, stating that you are a hard worker, who loves to get things done. You don't play around, and I love people who strive to work." He said, getting straight to business with her. Was he testing her? Saying she had an option. She huffed lightly, before glaring at him, before raising herself and leaning against his desk. She knew she was overstepping her mark, but didn't care.

"If you think I'm going to wait till Monday, you'd be a fool. Excuse me for being a little crass with you, *sir*, but I think you've tested my patience long enough. Don't you think?" She asked him a bit sarcastically, looking him dead in the eyes. Blue meeting hazel. He raised himself up to her eye level, so they were nose to nose.

"I think I've done what every CEO would do for their company. Make sure they have the right people working for the job. I could always

54

send you *back* to Texas, if you wish." He said to her, his voice a deadly under tone of don't tempt me or I will. She didn't know why, but she had a feeling that he was enjoying this. That this was a game for him. Well, two could play it couldn't they? She thought with a smirk playing on her face.

"If you send me back, you would regret it. Plus I rather be in this city, where I *originally* was supposed to be. Now, what floor should I go to so I can get to work?" She asked him, as she signed the papers, before standing up straight. She knew that she was getting under his skin, she could sense it. But he was doing the same to her. *Game on.* She thought wickedly, knowing that this wasn't going to be the only encounter they would have with each other.

"Twenty first floor, talk to Taylor Kelly. He's the head of the department. Have a good day, Miss Night." Sean said to her, still staring at her. She laughed lightly, before smiling sweetly at him, before walking away. She was going to love this job, not only because of her love for work, but because this CEO was going to be fun messing around with. If he wanted to play a game with her, then she could play back. She opened the door, leading out of his office, turned back noticing he was still standing there, watching her, almost as if he was staring right through to her soul. She frowned at the thought, before walking out without saying another word.

She walked past the two ladies, towards the elevators at the end of the hall, pressing the button to go down to the floor he indicated. She couldn't quite shake off the feeling of his eyes, his scent, and the way his muscles rippled through his suit jacked out of her mind. If he was playing a game with her, then why did she feel like there was something more going on. She shook her head, not wanting to read too much into it, as the doors pinged open as she stepped inside, pressing the button to the twenty first floor. She then got excited, wondering how she's fit in with all the other editors, as she watched the floors slowly tick down to the level she needed. And as the doors finally opened, she felt like she was finally at the right place to be, as she walked off towards the office of the head department manager and to her first day on the job.

CHAPTER 8

SEVERAL DAYS HAD PASSED by since that moment. Since he had met the girl that was constantly on his mind. The red hair, the piercing blue eyes, and the small framed body etched in his mind's eye. His dreams so real, he thought he could actually reach out and touch her. But he wasn't going to admit it to her, or anyone else. He had worked out over the weekend, to the point where he almost past out in exhaustion, but he had played it off like a champ so that he wouldn't worry anyone, especially his bodyguards. He was still not sure why David kept Charles around but he wasn't going to get into that. Let alone tell him what to do either. It was an argument he didn't particularly want to have either, his only hope was he knew what he was doing. After all, he had taken a three day weekend, knowing that today, being Tuesday, he would have to play catch up. Something he didn't particularly look forward to, but it had to be done. He groaned, as he turned to his side, looking at the clock on the side. It was *nowhere* near time to wake up, but his mind wouldn't shut off. It seemed to run scenarios of what could happen if he approached Emily, to being slapped by said woman over and over again. It was annoying and frustrating at the same time! He sighed feeling his muscles scream at him as he sat up. He had definitely over did it the past few days! He thought to himself, rubbing the sleep out of his eyes. It was pointless to even try to catch a few more hours of sleep.

He got up, putting some sweatpants on that we're on the chair next to the dresser. He still wasn't sure why he kept the damned thing in here, but it came in useful for the sweatpants or workout clothes he would place on it. It was easy access anyways, as he padded his feet across the cold floor, before opening up the door to the rest of his place, and down the hallway towards his office. It was almost four in the morning, but if he wanted to play catch up, he'd have to do it from home first. He opened the door, turned on the light, before sitting down in the black roll around chair, as he turned on the TV to a music channel. He didn't really care what it played, as long as it wasn't cheesy and corny. The beat of *Barracuda* by Heart started up. The tempo making him drum his fingers on his desk, as he leaned back and closed his eyes, letting the song wash over him. Oh how he loved classic music!

> So this ain't the end - I saw you again today
> Had to turn my heart away
> You smiled like the
> Sun - Kisses for everyone

His hands were on her body, rubbing her sides, as he kissed her hard and powerfully. Her scent strong in his nose, making him ache to touch. To rip all the garments off of her person. She smelled sweet, like she always did. Her fingers running down his naked arms, his shirt at the waste still tucked into his pants. She broke away from the searing kiss, placing feather light kisses along his jaw and then down his neck and chest. He groaned as he stopped her. He saw the look in her eyes, they seems even bluer than normal, before she raised her hands up, letting him take her shirt off. She wasn't wearing a bra, which made him chuckle. His erection digging into her crotch.

He opened his eyes immediately, looking around the room, seeing that he was by himself. He gritted his teeth, before sighing. It was going to be a long ass day, especially with his erection that was wanting to spring free from its clothed prison. He changed the channel, to the news, trying to distract himself. But it felt so real, as had the other dreams he had of her. He shook his head, before thinking of *anything* to will his hardened member to soften. It worked, but for how long he wasn't sure. Turning on his laptop, he decided that work would help him be in focus. And once it was booted up, that is what he did.

A few hours went by, it was time to get ready for the day. He walked past the breakfast island, where the house maid was busy at work, the smell of oatmeal and toast filling his nostrils, as he made it to his bathroom. Turning on the hot water, he got under the spray and stood there letting it scorch his body. The steam slowly filling up the room. His mind wandering back to her, as one of his hands decided to rub one out in the shower. He knew he was safe on his floor at the office, seeing as only important people came up there to see him. At least he hoped she wouldn't go up there, as he came on his hand hot and hard, the water already washing it away in the heat of the shower. He then stepped out, dried himself off, and got dressed. He decided a one piece suit, a greenish hue with a slight tinge of brown in it. He thought it bring out the color in his eyes, as walked back out into the main area of the house.

He noticed David was standing by the window, watching the rain fall from the sky, before looking towards him. They both nodded their heads at one another, as he took his seat at the breakfast bar. His tired muscles aching all the while from overuse as he dug into the oatmeal before him. He moaned with pleasure, as he noticed it was his favorite kind. Brown cinnamon sugar with blueberries, as he turned his head as he heard the laugh come from his right. David knew he always did this, but Charles however didn't. He shook his head, as he gave the kid a wink. There was nothing wrong about appreciating food, especially if it was one of your favorite foods to eat for breakfast.

"Boss you going in today?" Came the kid's question, which made him laugh. Of course he was, but even so he probably never thought he'd see him take an extra day just to relax and work out. David had seen him do it before, but it was a rare thing. A *very* rare thing. He turned to him, with a smirk on his face.

"Nope, I figured I get dressed for no reason and pretend to work today. Hell, I might even go skinny dipping in the pool for good measure." He replied sarcastically, as he chuckled by the look the younger man had on his face, before ruffling his hair up. "Don't be naïve, yes I'm going in today. I'm the boss, I'm allowed to play hooky." He said matter of factly, as he got up from the stool and placed his dishes into the sink. Running some water over the bowl, so that the left behind oats wouldn't stick to the bowl. He walked over to his office, grabbed his laptop, and briefcase, and headed out of the room. Both men were waiting for him outside as he got into the backseat.

He knew he'd regret it later for not shaving his face, but for now he wasn't going to worry about it, as the car was started and headed out to the city once more. He looked at the papers, that he printed out, as he placed his laptop into the briefcase. They were over the quarter earnings, which had been higher than ever thought imaginable. A lot of great books were being published, some of which he had read a few chapters from. He was very happy about the news, as he looked when he felt the vehicle slow down, traffic as always picking up. He turned his attention back to the paperwork, marking some things out that didn't really need his attention. He yawned a little, noticing the rain was coming down harder, and took a swig of his coffee that was next to his seat, as he dug himself deeper into his work that he never noticed, until the door opened that they had arrived at the building a little while later.

He got out of the car, after placing the papers back inside, and headed inside. Luckily for him, the garage didn't leak and having curbside service was a plus to him. He headed towards the elevators, while looking at one of the papers he had dug out of the side pocket, re-reading it over. He didn't look up, till he almost ran into someone.

"Watch where.... Oh." Came the voice of Emily. The one person he was *hoping* to avoid, or try to at least. It was no use now seeing as he ran into her, but it had been his fault anyways seeing as he wasn't paying attention to his surroundings.

"Emily. Nice to see you again." He said to her, with a brief nod before giving her a brief nod and walked off towards one of the opened elevators. He was thankful that there wasn't a lot of people around or even on it. He didn't need to be asked a million questions as to why he wasn't here yesterday, or the latest gossip. He would've been here earlier, if it hadn't been for the weather or the traffic jam. The doors were about to close, when a pink heel stopped the process. It was her, he knew it even before he saw the rest of her body.

"So is that how you are with your employees, *Sean?*" She asked him, as the doors closed behind them. Her arms crossed, as she tapped her foot on the tile. He stepped forward, pressed the emergency stop button and stood face to face with her, with a smirk playing on his face.

"It's Mr. Bowling or sir to you, Miss Night. I am late to work this morning, seeing as there was a traffic jam on the way in, but so are you. Wouldn't want to get written up now would you, especially with it being your first week?" He asked with a smirk on his face, challenging her. It was just a game, a game of who could take it higher till one or both of them broke this little charade. But either way he was enjoying it, she stepped closer to him, their noses almost touching, her breathe tickled his skin but he didn't show her that it affected him. He couldn't give in. He wouldn't, as he looked her up and down, noticing the slight cleavage from where he stood.

"It's only because of *the ass* that is standing in front of me is making me late." She said to him, glaring at him before she stepped away from him and towards the buttons on the wall. The tension could be cut with a knife as the elevator ascended upwards to the higher levels. He wanted it to stop again, but knew that more time would be wasted if he did that, and as the doors opened to let her off on the twenty first floor. She looked back at him, giving him a deadly look, before walking on as the doors closed to take him to the top level. He let out a sigh of relief, wondering how he was going to make it through this day without having a permanent hard on. She was so close to him that he could've kissed her, but even he knew it was too soon for that. He immediately shut that thought down. It *couldn't* go anywhere. She probably didn't even like him the way he did her anyways.

The doors then opened up to his floor, with a small ping, and he made a straight beeline walk over to his office, not even bothering to talk to his PA's. He knew he had to play catch up, and now wasn't the time to gossip with them. Not that he did anyways, but now wasn't the time to hear drama or who had the latest fashion tips. Some things he just didn't care to know about, as he opened up the doors to his office. He then sat down at his desk, after turning the lights on, and got straight to the pile of paperwork he had on his desk. He didn't bother taking out his laptop, because he had already answered all the emails on it, or the ones that he thought needed his attention this morning when he couldn't sleep for shit. He now realized why he didn't take days off all the time, or vacations for that matter. Work always seemed to pile higher than ever before, and his PA's could only do so much that didn't need his signature. The majority of which was here needed it anyways. His mind instantly putting Emily at the back as he got into full blown work mode. He knew he needed to get his head back in the game, or he would make some costly mistakes and he couldn't have that at all.

He was so engrossed with all the paper work, that the knock on the door, that happened a few hours later made him jump. He looked up, noticing that David was holding onto a baggy that looked like he had went down for lunch and had thought of him. He nodded his head, but didn't say much else as he went back to the papers before him. He sighed, noticing how many empty spots there was in a few departments. Some that happened to be key essentials for his company. He would need them filled up and quick, he wouldn't take any excuses either. He made a company wide email, for all the head departments, basically informing them to get off their lazy asses and find people for the job or they'd be fired. He didn't say it like that but he knew they'd get the memo. He looked up, as a clap of thunder sounded with a flash of lightening following. He frowned, noticing from the window the rain was coming down hard and fast. Standing up, he walked over to the window as another flash of lightening pierced through the sky, as the thunder rumbled loud and proud afterwords. He knew both of the girls weren't lovers of storms, Lucy being one big ole scaredy cat, he only knew because one time she had ran in his office crying heavily with streaks of makeup going down her face.

R. A. B.

"You ladies alright?" He asked them, after he walked out of his office to make his appearance known before them. He knew that he hadn't talked to them today, but the least he could was make sure they were alright, he wasn't always an ass like some people thought. The girls however both seemed to have it together, but he could tell that they were scared. He sighed inwardly, as they both jumped after another loud clap of thunder was heard several minutes later.

"Yeah, you know how Lucy gets though." Pam said to him, as the phone rang and said girl answered it and jotted some things down. He could tell, from the window behind them, that the rain was coming down even harder if that were even possible. He just glad he wasn't stuck out in it, like the rest of the city below him probably was at the time. He leaned over the counter, seeing all the notes cluttered everywhere, making him frown. How could they tell whose notes was whose? He wondered to himself, as he shook his head at the both of them.

"Clean this up. I don't get how you two can be so messy and don't blame the weather for such carelessness. I know I took yesterday off, so don't use that as an excuse either. We already know I'm playing catch up. So all this shit needs to be fixed ASAP!" He told them in a stern voice, looking at one to the other, as another boom of thunder roared through the sky. It sounded closer this time, the lights flickering a little. Thankfully they had a backup to the backup generator. He was prepared for such events, even though most in this building happened to panic when the weather turned south. He heard the slight squeak come from Lucy, making him roll his eyes.

"Can I go to the panic room?" Lucy asked in a small voice, making him groan in aggravation. The panic room was the worst place for her to go, seeing as you could hear the noise even louder, and he knew from past experiences that she would have a full blown out panic attack by being in that room. He shook his head, as the lights flickered once more. They turned off for a moment, then came back on. He just hoped no one was in the elevators right now. Last time they had a thunderstorm it took almost an hour to get the doors open for several trapped people inside. He just hope they would take the stairs, hell most of them needed to do that.

"No! You and I both know what happens when you go in there. So no. If anyone does come up here, make sure they have a valid reason." He said to them, shaking his head once more, before going back into his office. He saw David was sitting at the table near the back, away from the windows, jotting some things down on paper. He didn't notice him going in there, but he was more concerned about the clutter on the women's desk than anything else at the time. Walking over to the man, he noticed that it had to with security issues. Things he didn't usually understand, even though he tried to at one point in time.

"You like her don't you?" David asked, after he had gone back to his desk and got back to his paperwork. But the question made him look up at the man with confusion on his face. If he was referring to both women outside, then that would be a huge no.

"No, you know..." He stopped as the bark of laughter came out of the other man's mouth. Who was he talking about? He wondered to himself, as he rubbed his now itchy face. Oh how he wished he had shaved this morning.

"Emily. You like her." He said to him, walking over to him as he sat down on the desk. Both men looking at each other in the eye, as if trying to see what the other was thinking.

"You and I both know, David that I don't like anyone from here. I'm the boss, I have rules to follow...."

"Fuck the rules, Boss. I can tell you like her..."

"Even *if* I liked the girl, I'm not going to risk it. All any girl wants from me, is my money. I'm not going down *that* road again!" He told him, his voice becoming dangerously low as he stood up and clasp his hand on the man's shoulder. "I *appreciate* the fact that you *think* I have feelings for Miss Night but I'm not risking my life, or my fortune for anyone. So if you don't mind David, stay out of it." He told him with a warning voice, knowing he didn't have to say anything but use his voice to get his point across. He knew the man had his back, would die for him even, but he wasn't going to risk anything especially with all the past relationships he had ended up in almost losing everything he had.

"She's a good girl, I could see it...."

"Hush David! That is enough! I don't fucking care if she's a *good* girl or even the fucking president of the United States of America! I am **not** pursuing her. End of the damn fucking discussion!" He bellowed loudly, as another clasp of thunder rumbled loudly in the distance, lightening flashed making him almost sinister looking with the way things were going at the moment. The other man, opened hand closed his mouth wanting to say something back to him, but raised his hands with defeat. This was *one* argument that David wasn't going to win! He thought to himself, still raging mad that his bodyguard would even go there with him.

"You..."

"Don't even go there with me. Just fucking don't!" He told him, through gritted teeth as they both stared each other down. David sighed, shook his head at the whole thing, before walking over to the table grabbed his things and left the room. "Fucking ridiculous." He muttered out loud to himself as the lights shut off as the lightening lit up the sky behind him. He moaned with frustration, hoping that the backup generators would kick in soon or someone would be fired in maintenance! Minutes, hours seemed to tick by before the lights came back on, when really it wasn't that long after that they had kicked back on. He didn't dare go check on the girls right now, especially when his head of security was most likely out there, and frankly he didn't feel like talking to anyone right now anyways.

A few hours went by, when a ping was heard coming from his laptop. He had caught up, finally, with all the paperwork that he needed to look over from the past day and today. He opened up the email, noticing the annual banquet would be coming up this weekend. His thoughts immediately wondered to Emily, wondering if he should ask her to be his date, then shook his head at the thought of it. He wasn't going to ask her, especially when David would give him the utmost shit about it. He sighed, knowing that if he didn't get to know this girl personally, and soon, he's go crazy. He laughed out loud, at the mere thought of this, shaking his head and would just find a beautiful girl to take this Saturday. It wasn't important, especially when he knew all the ones he truly liked, in the past, had hurt him in the past. And he couldn't deal with that. Ever.

He opened up an email, pressing send to everyone in this building, and decided to tell them all about the upcoming event.

Dear Everyone,

*As you **all** know, the yearly annual banquet is being held on the first floor conference room. It will become, as always, a dance hall with live music, as we celebrate our yearly growth for the job we all do. It will begin at 7 o'clock and end at midnight, on Saturday night. Black and white attire. Dress your best, but nothing inappropriate! I will fire you on the spot, so don't even think about it!*

***Sean Bowling**, CEO of Books Bowling Publishing Inc.*

After pressing send he sat back in his chair, sighing as he yawned loudly. It had been a very long day and he could kill for his bed right now. Or maybe some vodka and rum, he wasn't really sure, as he rubbed his eyes. The storm had long since passed as he felt himself getting more and more comfortable in his chair, which would eventually lead him to taking a nap, and he couldn't have that. He texted David telling him to get the vehicle ready cause he was ready to go home, sure it was only a little after four but he had been up for over twelve hours now and needed his rest. He just hoped his dreams wouldn't include the piercing blue eyes of Emily Night or them having sex in various positions again, because if that kept happening he eventually wouldn't be able to control himself around her.

He shut his computer down, put it into his briefcase before getting up and made sure everything was in the correct order, before walking out the office. He waved to both of the girls, as he headed down the hall and towards the elevators. They knew if he ever left early, which didn't happen often, that they would have to stay till close and hold the floor on their own. He pressed the only button next to the elevator, and they opened up immediately as he stepped in them. He pressed the ground level and waited for the descend down to the floor. Thankfully, the doors didn't open on the way down, as he finally made it. He yawned loudly once again, as he walked to the waiting door and stepped inside. David closed the door behind him, before getting into the driver's side and drove off towards the busy streets of New York City.

CHAPTER 9

LIGHTS FLOODED HER BEDROOM, as the night life could be heard from down below, she hadn't bothered closing the blinds to her bedroom when she laid down on her bed. Sure, it had been a great first few days here in New York, visiting all the sites she could possibly muster over the weekend, even going to a few Broadway shows, but her mind was on constant speed. She was sleepy, but ever since she met the boss of the company it was as if she couldn't turn off her brain. The electricity was still buzzing through her, with a dull hum, as she turned on her side to look at lights that seemed to shine brighter at night. She wondered if he thought about her, or if he was too busy drowning in all the work he had to do, whatever that consisted of she wasn't sure. He was the big boss of the company and she knew it was most likely stressful, especially dealing with whatever it was he dealt with from the get go. She sighed, closing her eyes briefly, wishing to just get rid of him from her mind, but for some reason she couldn't and it was pissing her off, as she turned on her side to look at lights that shines bright in the night.

She sat straight up in her bed then, realizing that sleep wasn't going to come to her, before she looked next to her. The sleeping pills she refused to take every night, even though they were prescribed to her sitting there like a bump on a log. She groaned in frustration, as she picked up the bottle and opened the cap. Maybe this time, as she stared at the tiny tablet in hand, it wouldn't make her feel queasy and sick. There was no water however next to her, but it didn't matter she could dry swallow pills, even if it wasn't her favorite thing to do, she learned to do it when she was younger. Hell, she even faked taking pills as a child just to make her parents happy, but eventually got caught when they noticed what she was doing. She laughed at the memory, shrugging her shoulders, as she swallowed the sleeping pill dryly. She got up, closed the blinds, and laid back down hoping the pill would work this time without making her feel queasy or sick.

She didn't remember falling asleep, but she felt worse than she had done before. It seemed as if the pill only made her feel like shit, than it did to help her feel rested. She clicked her tongue, as she looked at the clock on the bedside table. It was only after six in the morning. She had only slept for several hours, but even so it seemed as if a rock was placed over her body making her feel worse than ever before. Getting up, she walked towards the kitchen to make her a pot of coffee, all the while feeling her feet drag under her. She was happy with the fact that she found a cheap coffee machine over the weekend, and it made some great coffee. She wasn't the greatest fan of the stuff, it tasted like nasty tasting cough medicine at times, but she took it like a champ and drank the stuff anyways. Once it was done, she poured it into her cup and drank it like it was, hoping it'd wake her up or make her feel better. If not, she'd stand under the scolding spray of hot water in the shower.

Her thoughts then drifted to Sean, as she walked over to her bedroom, wrapping a robe around her naked body, before heading back to the living room. She turned on the TV to a local program, as she wondered what he was doing. His hazel eyes came to mind, as she set the mug down and closed her eyes, picturing him in front of her. His ripped muscles taunting her, as he bent down to pick something up, smirking at her as he noticed that she was watching him. She sighed, wishing he was here with her, but *knew* he was off limits. There was no way he'd want a damaged beyond belief soul like hers anyways. She opened her eyes up, noting the clock was getting closer to seven. She had to be there at 7:30, the latest being 8 am sharp. She liked the head boss of her department, and elderly man with gray hair and brown eyes. He had welcomed her with open arms Friday, she wondered if he'd do the same today. She thought to herself, as she got up to get ready for the day.

She opened up her closet door, looking at the outfits she had bought over the weekend, before picking out a pant suit, which happened to be a Black Label by Evan-Picone with an open front jacket. She thought it looked great on her even if was nothing fancy just simple and to the point, before putting her hair up in a ponytail. She had no reason to impress anyone, hell she'd probably not see *him* again unless if it was by chance. And the chances of that were slim to none, even though she secretly hoped that she would. There was *something* about him that made her want him, more so than anyone else she ever had been with before. It was as if she was drawn to him, not because of his wealth but because of charisma. She couldn't quite place her finger on it, as she put her black heels on. The sun was just beginning to peak through the windows, as she made sure she had everything before leaving her apartment.

Once she got to the ground floor, where the garage was, she decided to take her Mustang to work. The taxi drivers she had encountered over the weekend had made her a bit nervous, so she decided to just drive the few blocks to work. She revved up her engine, as she went out into the busy streets of New York, seeing all the vehicles and people already walking to and from places. Oh how she loved this place, especially at night. It was the best! She thought happily, as she got stuck in traffic. It didn't last long, but to her it felt like eternity! She didn't want to be late or worse get fired, because of traffic, as she pulled up into the garage of her work. She drove around, spotting the empty spot that was supposed to be for Sean. Her thoughts immediately going to him, hoping he was alright as she found a place near the doors. She got out of her car, closed the door and frowned. *Maybe he had to be somewhere?* She thought, before shrugging her shoulders, as she made her way inside. It was Monday so it was bound to busy!

"Is Mr. Bowling in today, Kelly?" She asked, once she had gotten to her floor, and decided to ask him if he knew anything. It was bound to be all over, especially when his space was pretty close to the exit of the garage. The older man smiled, before shaking his head. For some reason that didn't make her feel at ease, only a bit worried, which was weird for her cause she didn't usually care all that much about her bosses health of mental state. But there was just *something* about him that made her want to know more about him.

"No, ma'am I don't think he is. You aren't the only one to have asked this question. I'm sure the boss is fine. No need to worry." He said with a polite smile, basically giving her the *'you may now leave the room'* speech without really saying it. She knew when she was being dismissed. It didn't take a no brainer on that to just know, as she nodded her head walking towards her own office. The great thing about this division, was she had her own office and not a cubicle like the Texas branch did. The people seemed to have welcomed her with open arms, which she didn't expect to happen so quickly, but they did. A few of them had asked her, on the first day here, if she wanted to go out for some drinks, but she had politely declined. They seemed to understand, as she turned the lights on in the room, leaving the door open as she sat down in her chair, noticing the paperwork and manuscripts that were already on her desk. She smiled, happily as she turned the computer on in the process.

A few hours had passed, as she read through all the papers. Placing things in the appropriate boxes, and even though the nagging thought of where's the big boss at was constantly on the back of her mind. A few times she wanted to email him, but she didn't think that was best idea. She got up, it was lunch time anyways seeing all the other employees walking past her now closed door. The blinds were open, so she could see out if she wanted. It amazed her that Taylor Kelly had put so much faith in her to put her in a quiet room, instead of the small cubicles that some of the others in the center had been at. *Must be Mr. Bowling's idea.* She thought to herself, before shaking her head at the idea. He didn't even like her, from what she could tell the first time they met.

Heading towards the elevator, she pressed the up button, the doors immediately opened and she pressed his floor. Maybe he had come in late, she only hoped, as the cart ascended up before opening before her. Her heels clicked beneath her as she made her way over to his personal assistants, both of whom seemed a bit worse for the wear. They both looked at her, with curiosity written all over their faces.

"Is Mr. Bowling in?" She asked, seeing as neither had spoken up. They sighed heavily, as she noticed all the papers that were in front of both women. For such a big space, they sure did seem to have made such a mess. She only hoped that he wasn't into such clutter, because that was an instant turn off for her.

"No, he took the day off. Which is a first in a while. Is there anything we can help you with though, Miss Night?" One of the girls asked as she walked over to her, with a stack of papers in her hands. She shook her head, raising her eyebrow at how much paper that was stacked in the small girls hands, wondering if she should help her or not, but wasn't sure if that'd be overstepping the bounds of not. But frankly she didn't see the problem, she was born to break rules. Or at least bend them as much as possible. It was a habit that she wouldn't let go.

"Want me to help you?" She asked her, nodding to the papers. The girl laughed lightly, before shaking her head.

"I have it. Well we both do. But if the boss does come in we will…"

"No, don't tell him I was here." She said looking at her then the other, with a small smile on her face. She didn't want him knowing that she was here. At all. "I best be going. Have a good day you two." She walked away, without waiting for a reply back as she headed towards the elevator. Pressing the button, she decided that it was best that he *didn't* know that she had come up here. She just hoped, as the door opened and she pressed the floor for the cafeteria, that they didn't mention it to the man himself.

The rest of the day passed by, with some amazing reads and some hilarious phone calls from potential clients for the company. She felt like she had accomplished something, more than she ever did in Texas, and was praised highly from Mr. Kelly himself as she had told him of some great potentials she had shared with him earlier in the day. She arranged her desk neat and nicely, before looking at the business cards that had been placed on her desk earlier. One that belonged to her, the other belonging to Sean Bowling himself. Everyone had them, just in case someone wanted to get ahold of him instead. She took his card, seeing his business phone and email on it. Of course his personal number wouldn't be there, that'd be an invasion of privacy for a man of his stature. She just hoped he was alright, seeing as things didn't seem right without him in the building. More people seemed to slack off, from what she could tell anyways, than they had been on Friday. She shook her at the difference a day could make.

She turned the computer off, got up from her desk, and grabbed her purse from the locked cabinet and headed out of the room after turning the lights off. Closing the door behind her, she noticed she was the last one around. It seemed like she was the only one that cared to work hard. Regardless if the big man was in or not. She sighed hoping this wouldn't affect the company or it wouldn't go to him in the end. Walking to the elevators, she noticed even Mr. Kelly had even left. *Slackers the lot of them!* She thought to herself, shaking her head, as the doors opened and she pressed the button to the ground floor that would lead her to the garage. She got to her car, noticing a couple making out in the distance near a Dodge Charger. She giggled to herself, but it seemed to carry out with an echo. They broke apart, looked around before looking embarrassed. It was one of the girls on her floor with a guy she had never seen before. She waved her hand at them, as she got into the car. She drove off, after starting up her engine and headed back to her apartment. Oh how she wished it was her and Sean doing that, but it was a dream. A dream she needed to stop envisioning especially after all the failed relationships she had in the past. One being the most recent. She be damned if she went through another *almost* rape or be cheated on. She couldn't take that.

That night however, her dreams were filled with hazel eyes. His body on top of hers, as he was deep inside of her, making her moan for more. His mouth on her breasts, sucking and biting them, getting them hard with desire. His arms wrapped tightly around her, as her hands clasped onto his ass bringing him that much closer to her, if that was even possible. She had woken up with a start, noticing that she had fallen asleep for once, and looked around the room. She was by herself, panting with need and desire, she could feel the moisture between her thighs. Laughing lightly noting that the dream had made her cum on herself in her sleep. Getting up from the bed she decided it was time to take a shower, it was a bit after five in the morning and it was useless going back to sleep anyways. The warm spray hitting her back, as she got in to wash away the dream. She only hoped he was there today. Unlike yesterday when he played hooky from work. She thought to herself, knowing that was probably not even the case. Sometimes the boss needed time to himself she was sure of.

She headed to the closet picking out a pleated faux leather dress, which came with pink heels. She wasn't too crazy about the pink, but either way she loved the dress. She just hoped that it wasn't too short. Hell, *some* of what the ladies dressed in was a bit questionable at times to begin with. They never got in trouble, but this was something she wasn't going to risk. She wanted her job, for all the right reasons, not because she had great tits or an amazing ass. She felt like that was how some of the women got their job anyways, but she wasn't going to be one of them. She decided to curl her hair some, noticing from the window that it was pouring down rain. She sighed, as she got her things and her jacket before heading out. She didn't bother driving today, getting into a taxi instead and heading to work.

Once there, she noticed that everyone seemed to be in a hurry to get to work. But then again they always seemed to do so every day. She placed her hands in her jacket pockets, as her heels clicked on the ground below her, as she headed towards the elevators. She was so engrossed in her own thing, that she didn't notice the person she ran into until the familiar electricity came running through her. It was *him*. He was here, looking a bit tired as a paper was held in his hand tightly. It seemed as if he hadn't been paying attention to his surroundings either.

"Watch where.... Oh." She replied finally, as the words just spilled out of her mouth even really noticing. He looked sexier with the stubble on his face. She wanted to touch his face, touch him *anywhere* really but she refrained from it knowing that it wouldn't be appropriate and would end up with her termination. His facial expression didn't give much away either, to her annoyance. He was hard to read, more so than any other guy she had ever met. It was frustrating!

"Emily. It's nice to see you again." He said giving her a brief nod, before leaving her behind. The electricity between them going away the moment he walked away. She narrowed his eyes, wondering what the hell just had happened as she looked at his retreating back. Was this *really* how he was going to treat her? Like some low life employee? She wondered feeling a bit hurt from the sudden thought.

"What an asshole." She muttered lowly, as she followed him towards the elevators. She usually didn't bother with chasing after others, but there was some type of pull towards him. As she caught up to the one that he stepped in, placing her foot in between the closing doors. He wasn't going to get away *that* easily. Not if she could help it!

"So is that how you are with your employees, Sean?" She asked him, as the doors closed behind them. Her arms crossed, as she tapped her foot on the tile, clearly showing her aggravation. He stepped close to her, as she could smell his scent and see his hazel eyes. They seemed to light up with amusement as he pressed the emergency stop button so that they couldn't move up anymore floors. For a moment she thought he was going to kiss her, but instead a small back and forth match took place. It was to the point where she wanted to strangle him. But two could play this game of his. A game that could either turn into something good or turn into disaster. And frankly she wasn't sure if she was scared or nervous or excited, or all three at once. The tension was so heavy between them, as she stepped back to make the elevator ascend back up to the upper levels, she wondered if it was always this way with him or just with her. Either way, when it reached her floor, she wanted to run out of the enclosed space and never look back. But that would give her away! She thought to herself, as she headed out and then looked back at him. A frown forming her face as he looked at her stoically back.

"It's just a game to him." She whispered to herself, feeling like she was being played without even being with him. She had been played like a fool in the past, and this wasn't going to happen again. It was just another reason to just keep to herself, regardless if the man was ridiculously hot and made her blood boil with desire, it just wasn't going to turn into anything. It was just a silly little game to him, as she walked into her small enclosed office and got to work. The rain hitting the window behind her as lightning flashed through the sky and the thunder roared loudly in the distance. Oh how she wished she was at home watching it fall there and not here instead.

The day passed on, with a slight interruption with the power going out because of the weather, but it went by smoothly for her. The email from the big boss had made her heart race like it had done earlier, in the elevator but seeing as it was an email for everyone and not just for her, made her feel like she had gotten excited for nothing. She knew it was useless thinking he'd ever personally email her. Let alone text her, especially when he didn't even have her number. She shook her head, knowing for a fact that he did when she had filled out the application she had to put it on there. The chances of him even bothering to ask her out for a date though was slim to none. He had better things to do than to ask her out. She sighed inwardly, needing something, *anything* really to take her mind off of him and all the other events that had taken place. The cops had called her, on her lunch break, informing her that Mark was going to jail for at least five years. Sure, she should've felt better about this, but even that system was corrupt. It worried her how the people in prison could easily escape. She never did trust the government.

"I don't even like the current president. Or anyone in the house or senate. A bunch of phony ass men who want to make everyone's lives harder to live." She muttered out loud to herself, before she realized the time. It was quitting time for the day, as she shook her head. How anyone trusted the government was beyond her. Always failed promises with even more failed dreams at that. Just thinking about it pissed her off, like it always did, as she got her stuff together and headed out for the night. Once she got to the apartment building, got dressed in something more comfortable, she decided to go for a drive. Where to she wasn't sure, but as she blasted the music in her car, she tuned out everything around her and drove. It didn't matter where, she just decided to drive and see where it took her in the end.

CHAPTER 10

IT BECAME A PATTERN it seemed like, each day they would run into each other and each day they seemed to have words with each other. He had almost pinned her against him, in the elevator that morning, but didn't. He however had a raging hard on since that time, and it was hard to work with. The rain had stopped around midnight, he wasn't really sure, as he looked out at the sun shining through the open window. It had been a laid back kind of morning for him, but he knew that would be a short lived thing. It was only a little after ten in the morning, as he made sure to keep quiet, his eyes fixed on the closed door, as he rubbed one out. He had almost gotten laid last night, but the girl wanted to be paid for it afterwords, which immediately turned him off. He had kicked her out of his hotel room, before she even had a chance to explain herself. He wasn't in the mood for excuses, as he stopped stroking himself mid stroke. The whole ordeal making his member instantly soft, as he zipped himself up. There was a knock on the door, as his next meeting came in. It was with one of the managers of a smaller branch who wanted to make an offer with him. He was still a bit iffy about the whole thing, but he had agreed to hear him out. He got up, smoothing out his tie, as he sat down at the round table to talk with him.

He had declined the offer, after a few minutes into the meeting. He knew it wouldn't help build his company up, only make it go down. He was aware of what happened to the last publishing company that jumped head first into the offer, they had sunk fast. And he wasn't willing to let that happen to his company. The elderly man tried to convince him, with no avail, as he shook hands with him and led him out of the door. He watched as the man turned the corner as he looked at both of the ladies. He just shook his head at them, wondering why he had agreed to let that man come here again. But it was these two women who wanted him to see it through. A deal he knew wouldn't happen, and even so he knew it wouldn't be the last he heard from him.

"Next time ignore that man's fucking phone calls. Waste of my damn time. Ten whole minutes gone, over such a shitty idea!" He said to them, knowing that he didn't usually cuss at them or around them, but they had acted if it was no big deal. He sighed as he walked behind the desk of theirs, placing his hands on both ladies shoulders. "Look, I know you had good intentions, but I know you know that he was a bit of a joke. And if you say otherwise, then I know you're only lying about it." He said giving them a playful wink, as he looked at the space before him. It was definitely organized compared to the last time he looked back here. He didn't really want to go off on them again if he could help it.

"He kept calling...."

"I don't care if it was someone from the national bank of some god forsaken land calling to see me, if you and I both know it was a farce. Got it?" He asked looked down at Lucy who seemed to be amused by his choice of words. He rolled his eyes before messing up the woman's hair, before looking at Pamela who was laughing at the way Lucy's hair now looked. He'd never understand why they took so long to do it for, when they hardly left this floor except when they left this area to go to other floors. It was rear though, but he loved their dedication anyways.

"You need to show..."

"If you say I should show more of my playful side, like I do with y'all then that's a negative ghost rider. Got to keep people on their toes, ladies. No need to let people think I've gone soft hearted now."

He pointed to the papers that he took from each of their piles and placed it in front of them. "Get back to work." He told them with a playful smirk on his face, as he headed back into his office. There was just no way he was going to let *anyone* see his playful side, unless he knew them. It wasn't a common thing for anyone to see anyways, but it would ruin their image of him. He shook his head, as he walked over to the door, which led out to the balcony and opened it up. It was the last day of the work week, the event was tomorrow, and his insides itched to ask Emily as his date. But the rule he had made was set in place for a reason. Not to be broken. He sighed inwardly, as he looked at the scenery before him, hearing the faint sirens in the distance. He wasn't sure if it was the police or fire department, but either way there was always something going on in the city to warrant the sirens to sound. He watched as the birds, on the roof across the street, were fighting over something and noticed the boats in the distance. He needed to take his speed boat out for a spin sometime, but something always seemed to come up. He knew it wasn't an excuse but still it did seem like something always needed his attention no matter the time of day or week.

He walked back inside, closing the door behind him, as he sat down at his desk getting back to his paper work. There wasn't much, but he wanted to stay ahead of the game, as a long sounded coming from his laptop. He typed his password in, before clicking on the email icon. It was from Emily, but there was no subject header. He scratched his chin, debating on whether or not to open it or leave it be, but in the end he decided to look at what the infuriating woman had to say to him.

Hello,

Can I speak with you on my lunch hour?

*Emily Night, **Editor of Bowling Books Publishing** **New York City divisional branch***

He looked at it several times, before wondering what it was that she could possibly say to him. He looked at the time on his laptop, noticing it was a quarter to noon. He hit the reply button and typed a message back to her.

Well hello there Miss Night,

*Nice to see you know how to message **me** back. I was afraid you didn't know how to use such technology. As for seeing you on your lunch hour, well I'm happy to say I'm available. So do come up here to my level.*

*Sean Bowling, **CEO of THE Bowling Books Publishing Inc.***

He hit reply, laughing at his own self at the choice of words he used, as he beeped the girls outside that she was coming up. They didn't say much, not that he was expecting anything back anyways, as he went back to the paper that he was working on before he had been sent the email. Not too long after he had sent the email to her, he heard the knock on the door, and in walked said woman herself. He nodded at Pamela, indicating she could close the door behind her, as he sat back in his chair, steepling his fingers together. A smirk playing on his face, as he looked at her.

"Ahh we meet again, Miss Night." He replied with sarcastically at her, as he watched her walk towards him, as she sat down on his desk with a raised eyebrow. He just stared back at her, wondering what was so important that she had to come up here on her lunch hour. He was a busy man, he didn't have all day long to play the staring game with her.

"Do you hate me or something? Is that why you act like a royal asshole to me?" She asked him, after several minutes of tension filled silence. It was always surrounding them, like a plaque. He chuckled as he leaned forward, touching her kneecap as he did so. He was trying so hard to ignore the electricity that flamed through him at the slightest touch. But it was getting impossible, seeing as it was there. The fire that seemed to inch through everything. Maybe that was why he acted the way he did towards her. Or maybe it was cause of the thrill. He sighed inwardly wishing to be anywhere but here, alone. Alone with such a fiery spirit, who seemed to challenge him no matter how many times they saw each other.

"I don't hate you, Emily. Why would you even ask such a thing?" He asked her, slowly standing up, as he looked her dead in the eyes. Piercing blue meeting hazel. He was taking a risk as his raised a hand to her face, lightly touching her lips, all the while asking with his eyes if it was okay. He was going to break the rules. It didn't matter, as long as she didn't become a gold digging bitch.

"Yes." Her simple small response came. The unasked question that wasn't even asked was left hanging in the air, as he raised his other hand to her face; cupping it. Their eyes locked briefly before he leaned and kissed her. The moment their lips touched, it was if an explosion of fireworks went off, the kind you saw on big events. It was something he had *never* experienced before. It scared him, as he pulled back, noticing that something else was at an attention; his dick. He sighed inwardly, knowing that it wasn't the exact moment to have a hard on but he couldn't resist. He heard the small giggle come from her, but nothing more.

"I'm.... was..."

"No it wasn't."

"You sure you weren't trying to seduce me?" He looked at her, trying his best not to touch her soft lips against his fingers or lips again, but she leaned forward giving him a peck on the lips as she cupped him. He groaned a little at the feel, before shaking his head, even if it did feel great. It was a little too fast. "No. No. Stop."

"I... just thought..."

"You thought I wanted you just for sex? No. You make my blood boil. I want to know you more. But I have this rule..." He stopped before stepping away from her, instantly feeling the connection leave. He didn't want to hurt her, but he also didn't want to start something that would eventually lead into heartbreak. He wasn't going to risk getting hurt, even if they had some kind of connection between them. He could see the instant hurt in her eyes, before she hid it from him. But he knew that she was hurt, something he wanted to avoid at all costs.

"You can break your own rules, Sean. But I should go. I've wasted both of our times." She said to him, the defeat evident in her voice. The spark that had been previously there in her eyes, gone. He watched as she got up from his desk, giving him a soft peck on his cheek, as if she was admitting to herself that nothing was going to ever happened. He closed his eyes briefly, wondering if he should go after her and take the risk or not then regret it later on. He couldn't believe how torn he was at the whole situation!

"Wait. Stop." He said, as he saw her almost up the door. He walked over to her, turning around so fast that they were body to body, chests heaving at the same breathing pace, and their eyes locked with each other's. "I'll give you one chance. That is all." He said to her, his breathe tickling his face, before diving right in and kissed her hard on the lips. All the pent up frustration that he had for her since he met her last week. She broke away from the kiss first, their eyes locked before they both broke apart. There was a knock on the door, indicating that someone was up here to see him. He ran a hand down on his suit, calming himself down. It was going to be hard now this beautiful woman was his, but then again he didn't really ask her out either.

"Your next meeting will be here in ten minutes, sir." Said Lucy as she looked at him, than at Emily and back again. He cleared his throat, looking at her with a pointed stare, as the latter blushed with embarrassment and closed the door behind her. He heard the giggle come from Emily once more, making him smirk. He took her hand, leading her over to his desk, as he picked up a pen and tore a piece of paper off from the notepad that he really used.

"Here's my number. If you want to text me, use this. Not the company computers. They are all monitored and it'd be mess...." He stopped talking, when she placed her hand over his mouth.

"I figured as much. I'm a smart woman, sir. Have you seen my GPA or the work I've turned in the past week? If not, I'm sure you'll enjoy reading my stuff." She said in a sarcastic way, before briefly kissing him, as she tucked the note in her purse. He shook his head, before giving her a gently pat on the butt when she turned around. Oh how he could watch her all day long if he could, but he couldn't seeing as they both had to work.

"Behave yourself now, Miss Night. Talk to you later." He said with a wink, as he leaned against his desk. She rolled her eyes at him, before opening the door and leaving his office. He sighed, hoping he wasn't going to regret this later on. All his past relationships had ended up the same way, they all wanted his money for some reason or another. And even though there was something different about Emily he was going to still hold her at arm's length, no matter what.

The rest of the day however, went smoothly. Even though, there had been a small fire in the lounge on one of the floors, that had been put out immediately. He had to deal with that nonsense, especially when the man seemed to have seen no foul play in the whole thing. However, he had been one of the men on his list that was getting close to being fired anyways, and by the time he smarted off at him, he was terminated on the spot. Which in turn, had led security to escort him out of the building. He rubbed his forehead, just thinking about it, before looking at the time on the clock. It was near seven at night, he had stayed an extra few hours to get everything situated and sorted, especially after the situation. He yawned, before shutting off his laptop and stood up once he tidied up his things, as he got up looking around the room and headed out of his office. Both of his PA's had left an hour ago, giggling about the upcoming event tomorrow night. He shook his head at the conversation they had at the time, and headed towards the elevator. The doors opened and he pressed the button leading to the ground level.

"Good evening, Mr. Bowling." David said as he opened the door to the back. He nodded his head as he got inside the vehicle. The man knew about him and Emily, had just smiled but said nothing more, as he watched him get into the driver's seat and drove out of the parking lot. He took his phone out of his pocket, seeing there was several texts from different people, but none from Emily since earlier that day. Another reason he liked this woman; she wasn't pushing him to talk and giving him the space that he needed. He wasn't one for a clingy girl. It only made him want to strangle them, even though he never laid a hand on one he had been tempted at times.

> S: hope your day went smoothly ;)
> E: besides the smell of smoke, that came through the vents, and some asshole firing the asshole that did it. Then yes, it went very smoothly. ;)
> S: shame you deal with such people, Em.
> E: I know right?! xD
> S: see you tomorrow night?
> E: I'll wear something so skimpy that your dick will fall off. ;) ;)
> S: then you will get fired. Wouldn't want that now would you? ;)

The fact that the entire conversation had him smiling like a crazy person was one thing, it was another to see that she was going along with it. Maybe she *was* different than the rest of the girls he had ever been with, but even so he had to keep his heart guarded. It wasn't every day that a man of his stature could just... find somebody that challenged him. Wanted him for him, with no strings attached, no hidden agendas, and no one on the side to be there for them when they didn't work out. He didn't get why girls were so shady about things, but men could do the same thing as well. However, he wasn't like that and didn't plan on it either. He just hoped that this was the right thing, that she wasn't some crazed psycho manic who killed people in her sleep, or was pretending to like him just for her own good graces. He sighed, as he thought of all the scenarios they played in his head as he watched the lights pass by him.

CHAPTER 11

LOOKING OUT OF HER window, seeing the vehicles go by, was something she was beginning to enjoy doing when she couldn't sleep at night. It had started the day of the whole elevator banter that had taken place between them. Sure, she had kissed him. He had made the first move, but she was worried. Worried that this was a dream, just to wake up and realize it wasn't all real, but the way his lips felt wasn't made up at all. They were rough, but soft at the same time. His hands had felt soft against her skin, as she leaned her head on the window. A silent tear escaping from her eyes, as she closed them briefly. The night always seemed to play with her, give her thoughts that weren't quite right and didn't seem true at all. The fact that Mark was in jail, was a great thing, considering he got some years to serve there. But the system was corrupted, and it worried her he'd come back to do something to her. She gulped just thinking about that night all over again. He had been drunk, high on some type of drug, and wanted to rape her. She tried to block it out. Tried to pretend it never happened, but now. Now that she was with Sean, or supposedly with him, it made her wonder if he too was going to do the same thing to her.

She sighed as she looked over at the nightstand, seeing her phone light up in the semi darkness of the room, the lights from outside were the only thing giving light in the room. She walked over to it, pressing the home button to see what it was, it was Sean. The text however, was from earlier when he told her goodnight. She had pretended to go to sleep, even laying in her bed to will herself to sleep, but nothing came. It was impossible to pretend that she got a good night's sleep when she couldn't even get that but every other day or so. It had always been like that, no matter how old she was or if she had to work the next day. Her insomnia was ultimately going to be the death of her, she was sure of it. She thought to herself, before laying down on her bed, staring at the ceiling. She wanted to call him, but didn't want to seem like a crazed girl who needing saving, when in truth she felt like she needed it at times. Hell, it was everyone's dream, when they're little girls, to be a princess in a nice shiny castle with her prince on her arm. She laughed at the mere thought of it now.

She rolled on her side, closing her eyes hoping for dreamland to catch her. The sleeping pills sat on the table, ever so welcoming but she refused to take them. Not after what had happened the other night. The clock shined bright in her face, reading a little after three in the morning. Placing the pillow over her head, to shut all light and noise out from around her, she willed herself sleep. It was one way of getting some shut eye even if it meant just for an hour or two of rest. But it seemed as if her mind didn't want to shut off, but she left the pillow over her head and stayed like that till eventually her body slowly relaxed and eventually fell asleep.

The next time she woke up, the sun was out and the light was on her face the moment she took the pillow off of her face. She groaned, as she sat up in her bed, wrapping the blanket around her naked body, as she looked at the clock next to her bed. It was a little after eight in the morning, which made her smile. She had slept more than what she thought was going to happen, as she grabbed her phone off of the table. Pressing the home button she noticed her dad had called her. He never usually called her, unless he needed to speak to her, but then again he knew about her moving to New York, and probably wanted to hear about her first week there. She looked at the weather, seeing it was supposed to be a beautiful day. She immediately got up from her bed, took a quick shower, and then put on some comfortable jeans. She wanted to take her motorcycle out for a spin, it had been delivered to her apartment just yesterday, from where it had been placed in a storage house for a while, till she could get it back. She knew she needed to get ready for this event, for her job, but she *didn't* need all day to pamper herself, like half of the other women that looked like clowns at her job. It was crazy how some thought gobs of makeup on their face made her look great, it was the exact opposite in her opinion!

"Morning daddy!" She said over the phone, as she had grabbed her gloves and put them on her hands, before grabbing the keys to it and her helmet.

"How was your first week in New York?" came the deep booming voice of her father over the line. She smiled as turned her Bluetooth on, placing it in her ear, before walking out of her apartment. She didn't need her purse, only her license and debit card. It wasn't as if she needed anything. She just wanted to go out for a spin, spread her wings at least!

"Amazing! You know how I love this state. It's hell of a lot better than Texas!" She exclaimed happily, as she headed down towards the elevator and pressing the down button. The doors immediately opening up, she got in pressing G for the ground/garage level. Her adrenaline racing with excitement!

"That's good. Sorry to cut this short, sweetheart but I must run! Stay out of trouble." He said to her, chuckling as if he knew she wouldn't. Hell, he was her father anyways so he knew her real well, and knew that she always seemed to dig into some type of trouble. Sighing inwardly, knowing that not all the trouble she got into was the kind she wanted to face but had no choice.

"It's okay. You have fun being the badass that you are! Bye dad." She told him, as she clicked the button on her Bluetooth off, placing her phone in the side pocket of her ripped jeans, as the doors opening to the garage floor. Her dad, was a police cop in the state of North Carolina. Had been for years, and she was proud of him, even though he dealt with a crazy ass people, she knew he loved it no matter what. She put the helmet on her head, as she walked over to where her sports motorcycle was at; A black 2013 Yamaha YZF-R1M. It was super-fast, but she loved it just the same. It was her baby, and she had missed her! She hopped onto the bike, looking at her Mustang that was parked next to it. She rubbed her hand over her car, giving it a slight pat, before turning the bike on. It roared to life, as she revved up the engine a bit, before heading out of the garage. Placing the lid, to her helmet down, not wanting to deal with bugs in her teeth today.

She made sure to drive slowly in the heart of the city, till she got to the outskirts and winded up in the countryside. It was beautiful scenery, but this bike was made for speed and speed is what she wanted to aim for at the moment. She revved up, before zooming off, feeling the wind on her arms and body. She could literally cum on herself, from the vibrations of the bike, it wouldn't be the first time. Her thoughts immediately going to all the men who had motorbikes, which had admitted to her in the past, which had a hard time explaining their erections at times. She giggled, as she headed onto a highway and went faster, but made she it wasn't too far over the speed limit. Hell, she didn't really want a ticket again for doing that. Those fines were hefty and pricey, but she had a feeling they were even heftier fines here. But as she drove on, not really having a set destination, she felt freer than she had felt in a very long time!

It was a little after noon, when she made it back to the heart of the city, feeling tired but also wind burnt as well. She knew she should've put lotion on, before she had headed out, but she didn't even think about it. She parked her bike, placing the kick stand down, as she took off the helmet. A guy walking by, wolf whistled at her and she rolled her eyes. *Yeah, a chick can ride too asshole.* She thought to herself, taking her gloves off and grabbing her phone out of her pocket. A few texts from Sean, and a few missed calls. She should've told him about her plans, but it had been one of those spur of the moment type things, as she placed her gloves inside of her helmet and walked over to the elevator.

"Emily!" Came the voice of Sean over the phone, once she had called him. Her face lighting up with a smile, sensing the worry in his voice.

"Yes, that is my name. Don't wear it out." She said with a slight chuckle, as the doors pinged opened to let her inside the elevator.

She pressed the button to her floor, as she readjusted the ear piece in her ear. She hated these things, but came in handy at times!

"Em, why haven't you answered my..."

"I was on my motorcycle. It's been awhile." She interrupted him, in a sing song type voice. She became like a little girl when she talked about her bike. Even if it made people nervous.

"You're joking right?" He asked in a worried tone, making her laugh at the sudden way his voice dropped. Oh how she wished to see his facial expression at the moment. The doors opened to her floor, and she headed to her apartment.

"No, I'm not. She's my baby. I love my fast cars, gives me a thrill when I go for a spin!" She said to him, opening up the door to her place. She could sense his worry, even though he wasn't even here. She frowned, hoping she didn't already ruin whatever they had between them. But she wouldn't be surprised. Most men couldn't handle her enthusiasm for fast cars or bikes. It was something that thrilled her. No matter the cost, even if the constant worry of *what if* always played in her mind.

"I just.... I don't want to see you..."

"I've been banged up in the past. I'm a big..."

"Emily you know how dangerous..."

"Don't you fucking lecture me on..."

"I was worried when you didn't answer earlier. Now I'm even..."

"Stop fucking worrying about me, Sean. I swear... if you can't handle a girl on a bike. Then you must be a fucking bore in bed." She was red hot mad. How dare he try to lecture her on what she loved to do! She thought angrily, as she heard him sigh in aggravation on the other end. She could picture him undoing his tie, running a hand through his hair, as he paced back in forth. The thought made her smile some, but she was still fuming.

"I assure you I'm not a bore in bed, Emily. But the thought of you on a…"

"Stop while you're ahead, *sir*. If you have a problem, tell me to my face. I'm done with this conversation. I'll see you tonight." She hung up on him, without even a second thought, as she threw her phone onto the couch. She screamed in frustration, wishing he wasn't so quick to judge, as she threw her helmet with the gloves inside on the chair, taking her clothes off and taking a longer shower than she had done earlier this morning. "Fucking prick." She muttered to herself, as she washed away the dirt and grime from her body. She noticed she wasn't too badly burned, but she knew she'd have a pink tinge to her skin for the rest of the day. Luckily for her, it would turn into a tan later on, compared to others who looked like a tomato for days!

She wrapped the bathrobe around her after she had towel dried off, walking to her closet and looked at the dresses she had. Her thoughts went immediately to Sean, knowing she had been a bit stubborn about the whole thing, but she didn't want to have someone tell her what she could or could not do. It was one of her biggest pet peeves in the whole world. She sighed as she walked into the living room, got her phone off of the couch, and noticed he had tried calling her back several times. She gritted her teeth, before simply texting him her place and to come over, before heading back to her to get some clothes on. A beep came from her phone, a simple okay was the reply back. She rolled her eyes, as she walked into the living room to turn the TV on.

"Hi." She said to him, once she had opened the door and saw him standing before her. A look of worry etched on his face, which made her laugh.

"I saw the bike in garage. Next to a Mustang. I'm guessing that's yours too?" He asked as he stepped inside of her apartment, after she had opened the door a bit wider for him to come in. Closing it behind her

"Stop worrying…"

"Emily…"

"Don't. You. Emily. Me!" She said through gritted teeth, before being pushed up against the door and kissed roughly on the lips. She could sense his worry through the kiss, as they were teeth and tongue in a matter of seconds. Her hands were pinned against the wall, as he pressed his body against hers. She could feel his muscles ripple through his shirt against her body, his erection evident against her leg. She pushed him away slightly with her body, even though it seemed like it was bowing against her own will, but it seemed as if he understood, as the kiss ended a few seconds later and they were both panting for breathe. She giggled before she removed his tie. "Always so formal." She said with a smirk on her face, as she took a step to her left so they weren't so close together anymore. She wanted to just give in and do what her body wanted, but it wasn't the right time.

"I can let loose when I want to..." He stopped mid-sentence when she laughed out loud and shook her head.

"Oh really?" She questioned him, crossing her arms across her chest.

"Yes, I...."

"Show me then. Tomorrow." She said as if this was a challenge. She stepped close to him, staring straight in the eyes, as she ran her hands down his shirt, unbuttoning the first button, before biting his ear playfully. "I don't think you can." She whispered against his ear, before moving away from and sitting down on her couch. A playful smirk ever present on her face. She sat there wondering if the big dog could fit in her shoes for once, and for how long. That was if he was up for such challenge of course. She thought to herself, as she watched him walk over to her, sitting down on the table in front of her. Blue meeting hazel once more.

"You want me to rent out...."

"No renting out anything, big boy. Just the open road where anything is possible." She told him, not even liking the fact that he would even suggest renting out a place for a few hours or more. Was he that insecure about himself that he had to have a backup plan? She wondered to herself, as she bit the inside of her cheek. She could see the obvious worry in his eyes, but she wasn't concerned about it. She knew the rules of the game. Always did when it came to challenges, she *wasn't* a sore loser.

"Let me think about it. I'll have an answer for you tonight." His formal reply came, which made her roll her eyes at the response. Chicken shit is what he was. But she wasn't going to tell him that. Or at least not now of course. She leaned forward, kissing him briefly on his lips, before pulling away only so far so that his breathe tickled her face.

"I'll see you later then." She said giving him a wink, before taking his hand and raising him up off of the couch. "Time to leave, sir." She told him in a poorly British accent, which warrant a laugh from Sean himself. She winked, before swatting his behind, giggling as she did it, before leading him to the door. He leaned in, kissed her gently on the lips, before giving her hand a small squeeze. She opened up the door, watched him walk down the hall, before closing it behind her. She slid down the wall, till she was in a squatting position, placing her head in her hands. Hoping that he wasn't going to end up like the rest of the men from her past. She expected, at any time to wake up from a dream and realize it was just that; a dream. The way he made her feel, even though it was short and brief at times, made her skin light on fire. It was a good but weird feeling, but she was cautious at the same time. There was no telling if he felt the same passion or not, and she wanted to keep him at arm's length as much as possible.

She got up from the squatting position she was in, before heading back to her room to finally decide on what she was going to wear to this annual event. One that she had never attended before, especially since she was not one for dressing up for an event where half of the people acted fake anyways. She clicked her tongue, shaking her head at the thought, as pulled out several dresses and laid them on her bed. The constant nagging thought coming back to her of what if he was just using her? And only wanted a date for tonight just because. She sighed as she pushed the thought back and looked at the three different dresses on her bed, wondering which one would be the best for tonight's event.

CHAPTER 12

WORRIED DIDN'T BEGIN TO cover how he was feeling at the moment. He was nervous that she was going to show up to the event in some god forsaken fast vehicle that would eventually get her killed. He didn't even want to imagine that, but when she hadn't answered his phone calls or texts, he never imagined she was on a motorcycle on a free joy ride the majority of the morning. He gritted his teeth, as he stepped off of the elevator, walking over towards the sleek black Yamaha and could see how much of thrill it could be, just by the looks of it, but also the underlying danger. The Mustang shining brightly in its glory next to it. He sighed, knowing this girl was all about speed and being fast. Sure, he loved his fast cars too, but never imagined a girl to be one. Maybe that was a biased opinion of his, but the thought just made him a nervous wreck. Literally and figuratively.

He ran a hand over the handle bar of the bike, before doing the same to the rest of it. The power could be felt without even being on it. He could feel his head of security's eyes on the back of head, and when he turned around there David was standing with a look of worry and confusion. He knew he couldn't tell her the risks that were involved, he sensed that earlier on the phone. She was stubborn and a red head at that. He ran a hand through his hair, as he walked past his security and got into the back of the vehicle that was waiting near the elevator.

"Her bike, sir?" David asked, once he got into the driver's seat of the vehicle. He looked directly at him, and nodded his head at him. He could tell the other man was also worried, but when a girl was determined to do something, it was pointless to change their minds. He had learned that from past experiences with women he had been with.

"Yes, David." He said in a low tone, indicating he didn't want to talk about it as the drive off into the heart of the city. His phone vibrated next to him, thinking it was her, he picked the phone up from where it lay on the seat, noticing it wasn't Emily but from a previous ex-girlfriend; Isabelle. She had tried **everything** in her power to drain him of his money, pretended to be pregnant, and pretended to have broken a leg. You name it, she had tried it, but he had *always* been a step ahead. And in the end, she got nothing from him. He had gotten the best lawyers in town to work on the case. Frankly, she had been a pain in his ass ever since. He just hoped that she wouldn't come to tonight's banquet, *trying* to win him back with whatever new job she had done to her body.

He sighed, as he opened up the text that said *don't you wish you could hold these once more?* With an attached picture of her breasts, that were bigger than last time. It didn't turn him on, it only made him question where she had gotten the money from. Probably some fool, who thinks they're in love with the whore. He thought with disgust, instantly having a bad feeling for tonight. She was going to do something, what it was, he didn't know but he needed all his men to be on high alert. Even the new kid, Charles. It was already bad he was worried about Emily and her need for speed, but now more than ever to what this woman could do.

"D, remember Isabelle?" He asked, breaking the companionable silence as they made it out of city and towards where his place was on the outskirts of the city. He could sense the unease from David, within a few seconds of him asking.

"If you dare go back to that bitch, Sean. I'll rip..."

"Let me stop you while you're ahead. No, I'm not. But I want all my men on standby tonight. She might pull something off." He told him, handing him his cell phone at the stoplight they had just pulled up at. He could see the veins pop from the back of his neck. The girl was a thorn in their side, and this was like bringing up old wounds. David handed him his phone back, before dialing a specific number to get through to his team.

"Everybody on high alert for tonight, at S's event." He heard David announce over the phone, after he had heard Conner answer. He tuned the conversation out as he debated whether to text her back or not, but decided against it. She wasn't worth his time, but instead he checked all of his bank accounts. The personal, the private one, the off shores one, and the charity one. All of them checked out good, and he breathed a sigh of relief. He looked up, when the vehicle stopped once more, noticing they were at home. Getting out, he immediately went to his office and went straight to work. He knew David and the team would inform him of the details closer to time.

The hours ticked by, as he paced back and forth in his office after finding out more information about Emily's past. He had dug deeper into her past, especially after this morning, and noticed she had stayed in a hospital for a week due to wreck when she was younger. He had literally wanted to go back to her place, after reading the report, and wring her neck for such carelessness but he would never hurt a woman. He had never hit a woman before, and he wasn't going to stop now. But now he was even more worried, especially when she had told him to fuck off when he brought it up. Did she not care about her safety? He thought as he stopped pacing and sat at the edge of his desk, with his hands in his pockets.

He had thought back to the conversation, wondering if he should call her back, but the last time he had done that her phone went straight to voicemail. He knew she was fuming, he had sensed it over the phone and through her words, before she hung up. He had never dealt with such a fiery spirited woman before and it was driving him crazy. He looked up, when a knock sounded on the half opened door. It was his security guys, all six of them standing behind his head man. He waved them in, before sitting in his chair behind his desk. He just hoped Isabelle wouldn't do anything to jeopardize the already fragile relationship he was in even further. He already had a bad feeling about tonight, and he had half of a mind not to show up but knew that wouldn't be good.

"You have the floor, D." He told him, waiting for the man to begin. The door closed behind one of the men, who looked like more of a body builder than an actual security personnel. He wanted to chuckle at the thought but decided now wasn't the time to do it. The others were small in comparison to him, which was just as amusing. He faked a cough, as he tried to hide the laugh, but even David knew it was fake just by the look he had given him.

"Okay so as I've told you all, E is S's girl. If you see the boss' ex anywhere near her or even near him move in. I don't care if you have to tackle the skank down, just protect the boss and the girl. You three on my right will be at each door leading in and out of the room, and you three will patrolling. Don't take your eyes off of anyone, especially if they act suspicious." David told them, as he looked around the room at the men. His voice holding an authoritative tone, he was in his zone and as he continued on with the meeting. He didn't bother saying a word when David was in his zone. It just wouldn't be his place really.

After the meeting was over, he shook all the men's hands before going to his room to change into his tuxedo with a bow tie. He didn't really like them, but it was a necessity sometimes, but he still preferred a tie than anything else. He sat down on his bed, bent over to tie the laces of his shoes, before smoothing down his jacket. He walked out of his room to meet his head of security; the rest of the men had gone ahead to the building to make sure things were okay and nothing crazy was happening. They went over a few minor details, before waving goodbye to the house keeper. He had told her to take the night off, but she had insisted working. He didn't bother arguing with her as he got into the backseat of the vehicle. His phone rang, making him apprehensive at who it might be, and he breathed a sigh of relief when he saw it was his girl. *Hopefully she had calmed down from earlier.* He thought to himself as he accepted the phone call.

"Hey Em." He said carefully, not really sure if she was raging mad or not. He heard her giggle, the one that had become music to his ears, which made him instantly relax. It was only for a short while though, because he knew something was going to happen. The foreboding feeling hadn't left since earlier. He wasn't going to tell her though, there was no reason to worry her.

"I can't wait to see you." Was her short reply, but he knew she wanted to say more, but wasn't over the phone. He sighed inwardly, rubbing his forehead, as an impending headache was bound to happen at any second. "Look I took my anger out in a punching bag earlier. I'm thankful that I had remembered...."

"You have a punching bag. I... wow I..."

"I'm a tough woman. Yes I have a damn punching bag. It seems to me..."

"You're one challenging lady, Miss...."

"And you're an infuriating asshole who think women aren't meant..."

"Meant to be like men? How can you even...."

"How can I say that?" A heavy laughter filled the air, before a slight scream of frustration came on her end. "You've been with a bunch of boring ass women, Sean. For such a high profile...."

"I'm not boring. The last relationship...."

"Which was almost two years ago. She was a freak, I looked her up. Can't imagine why you didn't want a frisky cat like that around." She said teasing him almost. The last real relationship was Isabelle. She loved her playtime in the bedroom, almost to the point where they had stayed there for a day and half. But the fact of the matter was she used him. The whole entire time in fact, and her coming back *now* was a coincidence all in itself. He sighed knowing there was no going back, that ship had sailed. At least for him it had.

"It's not what..."

"I don't want excuses. I'll just see you when you get here." And with
that the line had went dead and the call had ended. He knew their
relationship had been put online, especially since they had dated for
nearly a year when the shit hit the fan. He wanted to keep it in the
past, but it seemed as if that wasn't going to happen. He ran a hand
through his hair, as he felt the car slow down. Looking up he noticed
the traffic was the reason, as it always was. He sighed, hoping that
Isabelle would stay far away from the event, but it was a yearly
event. Even some celebrities came to support it, but that was beside
the point. He looked out the window seeing the many lights fly past
in a blur of color, before they finally made it to his place of work. He
briefly locked eyes with David, as his door was opened from one
of the many events staff on hand. The flash of light temporarily
blinding him, as he ducked his head down and walked fast to get
inside. He hated the paps, with a passion. But he took it all in stride,
or as much as he could possibly stand.

He got inside, immediately talking to some of the men who had
purposely waited for him to come inside. They talked briefly, before
shaking their hands as he scanned the room for his girl, but couldn't
see her in the main lobby. He made his way, after being stopped
several more times, to the conference room. The biggest one he
had, and searched for her in there. He smiled as he spotted her,
the red shining brightly in the lights of the room, near the mini bar.
Walking over to her, he wrapped an arm around her waist, inhaling
the familiar scent of her.

"You look beautiful." He said against her hair, causing her to giggle
as she turned around. He looked her up and down. The dress had
a bit of a sparkle to it, if she moved in a certain way. It was a sheik
black dress that hugged all of her curves, which made him want to
take her into a separate room and have his way with her. But he
knew that it wasn't the right time, even though she radiated sexual
energy every time he saw her.

"So do you, handsome. But keep your hormones down." She said
teasingly, as she lightly touched the front of his pants, and feeling
his erection in its tight confines. He stepped forward briefly, as
someone passed by them, making her grab him for a split second

and released him. *Oh this was going to be a long night.* He thought to himself as he gave her a look of warning, trying as he might to keep her wandering hands from wandering any more than was needed.

"As much as I want to rip your dress off..."

"It's her...."

"What? Who?"

"Her." She said in a short tone, turning him around to face the other direction. He saw her at the entrance of the room, talking with several of his colleagues, and his eyes immediately drifted to his security who were all on high alert. He sighed heavily, as he noticed the bigger breasts, the heavy makeup pasted on her face, and the skinny figure from a mile away. Her hair was a shade of pink, with blonde and black streaks going through it. His fists clenched into balls, as she seemed to throw herself at the younger guys. This wasn't happening. He thought to himself, as he turned around to look at his girl. A look of uncertainty was there.

"I'm not sure why she is here. But no need to worry. I promise." He said, even though he wasn't convincing himself of the no worry thing. He kissed her briefly on the forehead, squeezing her hand afterwords. "I have to make my rounds. Get to know some people." He said, his tone becoming authoritative as he gave her a wink. He let go of her hand, before going to the front of the room to talk with some of his business partners. They were all talking about their latest bout in golf, none of them were good. He frankly didn't understand the game, and sucked at it. No matter how many times he played, he still managed to lose. Or was close to it. Either way he didn't truly know half of the time anyways.

He could feel her eyes on him, before he even turned around. He had tried for the past hour, as he made his way around the room, to avoid even talking to her. But he knew it wasn't going to last long. He heard the throaty laugh, one that used to turn him on but now made his blood boil with nothing more than complete loathing. She had been the one to make him not trust women. Especially when the ones after her had tried to cheat him out of his money among other things. He closed his eyes as she tapped on his shoulder, before turning around to face her. He could see that she had definitely changed from closer up. She was nothing like the skinny, b cup woman, who never wore make up at all anymore. It was like a day to night thing, a hooker in the making.

"Isabelle." He said to her, noticing out of the corner of his eye that his security were all in position to intervene if something happened. He could feel eyes on him, but the room was still loud with laughter and talking. She smiled sickly sweet at him, which made him feel even more at ease.

"Is that how you treat old friends. Like a..."

"You aren't an old friend, Belle. More like a..."

"Oh you're such a tease, Seanie. I'm only wanting..."

"If you think your fake breasts, and wannabe good looks will throw myself back at you, you are wrong." He said, as he stepped closer to her, glaring at her. She laughed sickly, as she stepped closer so they were almost nose to nose. Her perfume making him sick to the stomach, but he knew how to control it.

"You want me back. I can see it..."

"You're delusional. I wouldn't ever..."

"We will see about that, Seanie boy." She said with an evil smirk on her face, as she leaned in kissing him. She tasted of cigarettes and cheap lip-gloss, before he pulled away. He could see a red blob, from the corner of his eye, hurrying out of the room. He groaned inwardly, knowing he would have to do damage control with her later. But first he had to get rid of the whore in front of him.

"You and I have long been over, Isabelle Sundry. I don't give a flying fuck how badly you try to win me back. Or how low you stoop to do it. But we are finished. Have been for two years." He looked at Conner who was the closest at hand. "Take this bitch out of my site!" He bellowed, as he noticed David was not in the room. He only hoped that he went after Emily, he didn't want things to end between them just because of the bitch that was being dragged out of the room. The room applauded, as he adjusted his bow tie, as he looked around the room at the people around him. He noticed they were all the people that had watched everything unfold a few years ago. Some who hadn't, but he knew how gossip worked during the work week. He just waved at them, feeling unsure of what else to do.

"I'm glad you got rid of that hussy, sir." One of the men nearest him said. He laughed before shaking the man's hand. He still felt a bit uneasy about the whole encounter, hoping that would be the last of her. It was a wishful hope, as he walked up to the podium, his second in command was close by. The room went quiet.

"I'm making this brief. I appreciate everyone coming out, but I'm going to let my second in command take over. Enjoy the rest of your night guys." He said to them, before walking off the podium, and making a bee line for the door. He wanted to get to Emily's apartment, fix whatever it was she supposedly saw from her angle. He walked past all the people lingering in the main lobby, ignoring their calls for him, as he headed towards one of side rooms. It had a door that led to the outside, as he loosened his bow tie, feeling on edge at the whole thing.

He opened the door, after fumbling with the lock; it always managed to jam no matter what he did to fix the damn thing, as he stepped out onto the concrete. Closing the door behind him, feeling the sprinkles of rain fall from the sky, he walked down the alley and then to the left. He wasn't going to let Emily go. He had to *make* her understand, even though he wasn't sure if she would listen to him. She was a fiery spirit, that made his blood boil with want and she was beautiful, regardless of her dangerous habits. The sprinkles began to turn into rain drops, and he went into a jog as the drops hit him in his face hard and fast. But he didn't care, he needed to get to her, as he felt his clothes get heavier by the moment. The rain falling faster with each passing moment.

CHAPTER 13

IT WAS OBVIOUSLY A nightmare waiting to happen, she could sense it the moment that vile woman had set eyes on her man. He was obviously having a good time, but with the added security, and what she had overheard from a couple a few feet away from her, it was bound to end in disaster. However, she didn't think he'd step so close to her face, an hour later, to get his point across. She wanted to slap the both of them, her anger getting the best of her, but knew this wasn't the place for it. She blinked back the angry tears, as she saw the kiss happen. She wasn't sure who had started it, but it hurt. It stung even more than what it needed to. She thought, as she set the glass of champagne down, and almost ran out of the door. No one knew they were together, nor did the man who had sunk his lips onto the other woman. She knew to guard her heart closely, as she took her heels off her feet, and ran down the stairwell to the ground floor. She had taken her Mustang GT and once she got to the garage, she was glad. She could hear a voice, a deep one, yelling her name, but she tuned it out. All she wanted to do was get to her apartment.

She revved up her engine, feeling a lone tear escape and travel down her cheek. Not bothering wiping it away as she peeled out of the parking lot. She wanted to get away, far away as possible, but knew that'd be a moot point and would get her nowhere. She never noticed the vehicle following her, till she parked next to her Yamaha. The black shining brightly in the dim lights of the garage.

"Emily."

"You're not going to convince me that was innocent. I saw...

"The boss and Isabelle aren't an item. Never will..."

"Don't make excuses up for him. Just go." She said before sprinting towards the elevator doors, pressing the button to her floor. It immediately opened, and as she stepped in she looked him dead in the eyes, from where she left him at, daring him to make his way toward her, but he didn't. She gave a little wave, as the doors closed around her, ascending upwards to her floor. She closed her eyes, wishing she hadn't even gone to the event, but wanted to be there for Sean. It didn't do her any good though, as she only ended up heartbroken more than anything else. The door opened up to her floor, and she sprinted to her room. The heels making her feet hurt by the sudden change of movement. Growing in frustration, as she opened up the door, turning on the lights, she threw the heels at the couch. They missed, hitting the table instead, as she slammed the door, the walls rattling a little.

She knew she was overreacting, knew that he had the choice of choosing her of the other woman, but it didn't matter right now. No one wanted her, they always seemed to break her heart in the long run. It was too much. Too soon. She slid down the wall, not bothering to care if the dress ripped or not. Sure, it hugged all of her curves, made her breasts a little bigger, but it didn't matter. She might've gotten the approved statement from him earlier, but it probably meant something entirely different. A flash of light tore through the sky, matching her mood, as she noticed the rain start to fall from the opened window. She didn't bother closing the blinds before she left, there was no point when she loved looking out at the city. A clap of thunder boomed through the sky a few minutes later. She knew they got their usual storms here, but the weather pattern was pretty screwy lately to begin with. Hell, she couldn't imagine it getting much worse than last year's winter in the East. Though Mother Nature had a rather amusing way with things. So there was no telling how things would play out. A loud knock however interrupted her thoughts, as she could see how heavy the rain had gotten, in only a matter of minutes. She could watch it forever, from where she sat. She sighed heavily, as the knocking became persistently louder.

Getting up from the floor, she walked her way to the door, looking through the peep hole she noticed it was him. He looked wet and miserable. Had he run his way here? In the rain even? She thought a frown marring her features, as she opened the door to find him dripping wet, a small puddle forming at his feet. She wanted to say something, but words failed her. The obvious anguish on his face, the determined look, and the hope all written there. It was if he needed to explain his reasoning why he ran here, in the rain to be here with her. But it didn't matter at the moment, all that mattered was the fact he was here. He had chosen her, even though she wasn't really sure why, but it was in that moment she knew. She knew he didn't have to explain anything, because he wouldn't have gone out of his way to get to her, if he didn't think there was hope for them.

"Emily, I..."

"Shhh..." She told him, before pulling him inside, closing the door behind them. Their eyes locked, blue to hazel. A silent question passing between them as he turned her around, pressing her against the door, kissing her roughly on the lips. It was full of need and want, but always desire to be with her in an intimate way. This moment wasn't the time for talking, it was about them; connecting. Connecting without words, but with their bodies. She wanted to just rip his clothes off, but he had her pinned to the door, as he kissed along her jawline, to her left ear and then to the right. She raised her leg up, rubbing the obvious erection against the wet fabric. Her giggle sounding more like a moan when he playfully bite her earlobe.

"I want you. Have since..."

"The moment I stepped into your office? I could tell." She said with a playful smirk on her face, as he stepped back from her. She giggled once more, noticing the wet spot below them. "If it wasn't storming outside, I would've thought you peed your pants, sir" she said to him, before a loud clap of thunder was heard; making the walls rattle some. A lightning bolt lighting up the sky not even a minute later.

"Ha ha, Emily." He replied sarcastically, as he started to take off his sopping wet jacket. There was some parts of his shirt that were dry, but the rest of him was just wet. She could tell he needed her help, but the moment he took the bow tie off, she stopped him. He looked at puzzled, as she stepped closer to him. Unbuttoning the buttons of his white shirt, slowly but looking him straight in the eyes. She pulled his shirt out of his pants, going behind him and took it off of him. She noticed the tattoos on his back, tracing the Angel like wings on his shoulder blades, as she traced her fingers over them. He turned to face her, taking her hand, kissing the tips of each finger, before the center of her palm. She cocked her head to the side, as he did the other hand just the same. It felt different, but erotic at the same time. Her fingers trailed to his pants, unbuckling his belt, but he stopped her in the process, shaking her head at him. She glared at him, before he turned her around, thankfully her heels weren't on her feet or she would've tripped over her own two feet. He unzipped the zipper of her dress, instantly making it fall at her feet. The only thing she was wearing was her panties.

"Surprise." She said softly, her voice dripping with want, as he caressed her breasts fondling the nipples, getting them hard and perky. She placed her head on his shoulder, as she could get obvious arousal as he continued to play with her breasts. She turned around, capturing his lips with hers as she fumbled with the belt buckle all the while, but she finally got it undone and got it through the loops of the pants. It wasn't the first she had done this, while passionately making out with someone. The kiss however ended, their foreheads touching as they caught their breaths.

"Are you sure that…"

"I want you, Sean. I just…"

"Just what?"

"Don't want to get hurt, I've been…"

"Are you a..."

"No! I'm not, but..."

"I won't hurt you, Em." He said as if he figured out what she was trying to say, without her really saying it. She noticed however he was telling her the truth, just from his eyes. She was always told, as a little girl that the eyes were the window to someone's soul. And if she couldn't see the person, she could always tell from their voice. But as she zipped the zipper down, the pants instantly falling down to the ground with a heavy thump. The rain could be heard, in the background, getting heavier by the second as the thunder rumbled loudly in the distance. She looked behind her, turning off the lights, the lightening making things seem more real and sensual like.

Taking his hand, after he had stepped out of his shoes, and headed straight for her bedroom, but he had other plans it seemed like. He pushed her up against the wall, catching her off guard, but it made her realize he could be rough in bed. Their lips meeting in a sensual battle, as their tongues danced in a battle of who could win first. She pressed her body flat against his, bringing him closer to her as she grabbed his ass in the process. His obvious erection she could feel against her stomach, as he lifted her up. She wrapped her arms around his neck, never breaking the battle tongues and now teeth, as she wrapped her legs around his waist. She moaned into the kiss, as he fingered her moist entry to her pussy, as she could feel him move towards the opening of a room. A flash of lightening flashing brightly in the dark, making her open up her eyes as it happened again. Usually she didn't mind storms, but not when it was constant flashes and booming cracking thunder every five seconds. However, in the position she was in, it just made it seem more intense. More real and just that much more amazing. Breaking the kiss, taking a breather, his lips finding her neck and sucking hard; using his teeth and tongue. She knew there would be a hickey there, one that she'd have to cover up come the next working day, but it wasn't of importance right now. What mattered right now was them. She arched her neck back further, letting him have more access. His fingers causing her body to bow to him, as her skin seem to light up like fire.

She could feel him move, as he put two fingers inside of her pumping and pushing her to the edge, but stopped as she could feel herself getting close to the brink. She giggled, as he took her legs from around his waist and then her arms, before pushing her onto her bed. He wanted to play rough it seemed, as a bolt of lightning flashed through the sky, giving her dark room some light. She could see the smirk on his face as she sat on her legs, as he mimicked her, doing the same. She pushed him, making him fall backwards on the bed, and straddled him in the process, feeling his member pulse against her wet pussy. Bucking into him, she placed feather light kisses from his lips to where his chest hair met his belly button. He squirmed before he rolled her over, pinning her to the bed with his hands on her arms. She could feel his tongue bite, suck, and lick her breasts and then on downwards. Arching her back, she bucked into him again, until she was back on top again. She grinning salaciously at him, before she sat on his knees, before taking his cock into her mouth, sucking him fast and hard. The thunderstorm continuing on in the background.

"God woman..." came Sean's voice, through a breathy moan. She could tell he was close, just by the way he was bucking his hips up and grabbing her hair roughly. He pulled her up though, after her teeth graced the head again and swirling her tongue around the opening hole. He pinned her on the bed once more, before sinking his own teeth and tongue into her moist center. She cried out at the feeling, it was nothing she had experienced before. It seemed so right, yet so much hotter than ever imagined. Her hips gyrated in time with his bites and licks, her back arching and she cried out his name. No one, had ever ate her like this. No one had given it much thought to it, but thankfully she was shaved and waxed down there. It would've been embarrassing if she hadn't. She could feel the familiar rush, the pull, the tightening in her stomach as she knew she was near to release. The orgasm would be fast, hard, and a rush even. His tongue seemed to go in further, his thumb rubbing her clit in the process. Her skin felt over synthesized as she touched her breasts, tweaking her nipples, as she came hot and heavy into the man's mouth.

"Fuck!" She moaned loudly after coming down from her orgasm. She kept her eyes closed, as her breathed evened out, and when she looked over he lay there watching her. She knew he wasn't done, but the look on his face said otherwise. Had she done something wrong? She thought with a sudden pang of hurt, but as he kissed her briefly on the lips, tasting herself through the brief touch, she knew it was something else. She looked at him confused. A small smile playing on his face, he seemed almost shy and childlike before her. As if he wasn't this strong CEO everyone knew him to be, but a fragile one that had obviously been through so much, in the years he had gained power of his own empire.

"I don't have a condom." He said after a time, as their hands wandered over the others body. She giggled, turned over to open up the night stand, opening the drawer and pulled out a box of Trojans from the drawer. She gave it to him, with a sheepish smile, knowing he'd asked her where she gotten them, but instead he only chuckled.

"I hoped we'd get here.... eventually." She said to him, watching as he opened the box in front of her and producing one of the foil packets from it. She took the box, placed it on the stand as she turned back to him. She saw him roll the condom over his cock, and before he could say another word she got on top of him. But it seemed as if he was waiting for her to do just that, pinning her beneath him once again. She smirk, not wanting to be on bottom, and rolled them over again so she was on top. A look passed between them, a playful one, and she began to ride him. Their hands joining together, as she bounced up and down fast. She could feel him, everywhere inside and out. The thunder seemed to match the rhythm they made. The rain continue to pour in the distance, as the night went on. Their moans, mixed in with their names, filled the air as the storm raged on outside and inside the apartment.

CHAPTER 14

WARMTH WAS ALL HE felt, warmer than usual. He had been so used to waking up alone, but when he opened his eyes, a blanket of red hair was all he could see. The memory of last night, into the early morning hours, coming back him. It had been amazing even though what led them here however could've been different, but he was thankful that she hadn't thrown him out when he had shown up at her door last night. He moved some of her hair out of the way, noticing the marks on her neck. He groaned, not realizing how much he had attacked her neck, but she didn't seem to mind. He pulled her closer, fondling her breasts as a soft sigh came from the woman lying beside him. She turned over to her back, looking him in the eyes. He moved some of her out of her face, before running a finger down her face and then her body. Never once taking his eyes off of her.

He kissed her on the lips, as she started to stroke his erection with her hand. He groaned, loving the feel of her soft hand against him. He knew if this continued they wouldn't get out of bed for a while. Not that he minded, but he did have some business to attend to. Business that didn't need to be around anymore, even though the court had dropped his case about a restraining order against Isabelle, he still didn't want her anywhere near him or even Emily. He moved her hand from his erection, kissing her hand as a way of letting her know he was enjoying himself, but now wasn't the time. She seemed to understand, as she turned to face him completely, her hand holding her head up. He smirked, as he cocked his eyebrow at her. It earned him a giggle, a sound he loved to hear.

"Where'd you get the Angel wings?" She asked after a time, her voice low and whimsical like. He lifted up one of his shoulder blades, trying to see the tattoo, even though he knew he couldn't. He traced her palm lazily, knowing there had to be something else she wanted to know then that. But for now he'd play it her way.

"I had a past. Like..."

"Cut the crap, Sean. Get to the point..."

"Or what? You're going to unleash the dragon..."

"How'd you? I mean..."

"I didn't have sex with a ghost last night, Em. I saw the birds on the middle of your back. Now where..."

"I was sixteen when I got it. Thought it was badass. Now the wings. Or do..."

"I was twenty one, wanted the wings for..."

"Not buying it." She said to him, as she sat up in the bed. He sighed inwardly as he sat up, putting his arms around her and kissing her neck. Breathing in her scent, he could see the view of the city before him. The buildings went on forever, and he wondered if this was why she left her window curtains open, or just she had forgotten. He rubbed her back, noticing the tiny birds that seemed to surround some flowers, which went up her back to where a tiny scar was it. He touched it, noticing the small shiver that went through her body.

"What's the..."

"It's a scar, where I broke my back." Was the short reply, as she got up from the bed. He wanted to say something more, but figured it wasn't probably the time for it. He watched as she put a bathrobe on, covering her beautiful body. He watched as she went into the closet and brought some clothes out, placing them on the bed. He looked at her puzzled, wondering what she was doing with men's clothing, but he figured it had to with the motorcycle.

"So the birds and flower represent what?" He asked after he watched her put the clothes on, then walked out of the room then come back. His clothes, from last night, were in his arms. She threw them on the bed, landing with a heavy thump. He knew they weren't really dry, but he understood then. She was going to have get on the bike with him. Something he wasn't so sure about, but he wasn't going to voice his opinion on that right now.

"Put them on. They're a little damp, but we're going for a ride." She said to him, with a childish glee in her eyes and in her voice. He chuckled a bit, before getting up out of the bed and went over to her. He ran a thumb over her bottom lip, before kissing her on the lips. He couldn't get enough of her, which worried him a bit. He wondered, as she bit his bottom lip, how he'd be able to concentrate at work with such a beautiful woman such as this, working only several floors below him. He knew that he couldn't mess this up, but also he didn't know how much he could trust her either, especially with his past coming into the light. He broke away from the kiss, before it could go any further. He smiled at her, before squeezing her hand and put the semi wet clothes on. His phone, among other things seemingly were dry; though he was pretty sure his was fried from the rain last night. It was amazing it even turned on, but he texted David to let him know what was up.

Once they were both dressed, he followed her out of her apartment, and down the stairwell. He wasn't sure why she didn't bother using the elevator, but didn't question her motives as they reached the ground floor. She gave him a helmet, which by the looks of it hadn't been worn much; besides the few chipped areas that the paint was coming off, and placed it over his head. He watched her do the same thing, before hopping onto her black Yamaha motorcycle, and revved up the engine. He could feel the vibration of the machine to the tips of his fingers, as he got onto the back and placed his hands on her hips. He wasn't sure where they would go, but for now he'd trust her. He watched as she revved up the engine once more, before peeling out of the space leaving a smoke trail in her wake. He chuckled to himself, knowing she was just showing off for his sake, as she headed out of the garage and onto the streets.

As they pulled up to a stop light, he fished his phone out of pocket seeing that David had write him back. He didn't say much back to him, but he knew he would be watching from a distance along with his team. He felt safer just at the thought, but didn't let his guard down, as he put the phone back in his pants pocket. He felt a bit over dressed, especially when he could feel eyes on him, but it didn't matter, and at least the helmet hid his true identity. He held onto her waist a bit more, as she headed out to the outskirts of town, and into the country side. The wind picked up, as the bike picked up more speed, and his fingers held onto her a bit tighter. The feeling of freedom, everything he stood for, seemed to fall off his shoulders as he rode on the back of the motorcycle. He wasn't going to admit that be understood her reasoning, even though he never asked her questions about it. But he could see why, as pastures and meadows of small countryside town rolled on by, it was something she loved.

They stopped, however, on the outskirts of Albany, New York. He didn't realize they had come this far out, till she had stopped at a gas station, to fill up. The vibration of the motorcycle tingling his whole entire body, as he walked around. He looked at his phone, noticing that David was calling him, he pressed the accept button after taking the helmet off of his head, and set it on the ground next to him.

"What's up, D?" He asked, immediately going into business mode; his eyes looking around for any signs of immediate threat. The other man laughed, which he took as several different ways but didn't bother saying anything for the time being.

"Just wondering when you'll be back. We would like to debrief about last night." Came David's voice on the other end. He sighed, watching as Emily came out of the small store carrying a bag of sunflower seeds in her hand. She motioned at him, as a sigh of let's go. He has no other choice but to cut this joy ride short. Not that he wanted it to, but his life wasn't going to be put on for anyone, even if it meant her as well.

"I'll be home soon. Just hold your horses." He said to him, as he walked back over to Emily, as he hung up the phone. Putting the helmet on his in the process. He texted the directions to his house, without saying a single word, which made her frown as she kicked the bike into gear. She put her helmet on, as he put his hands on her sides, as she drove onto the road fast and hard. He had a feeling, as he watched her put the coordinates into the GPS on the dash, that she was going to show off even more now. He gripped her sides tighter, as the roared down the road. He noticed other bikers out on the road, who seemed to have joined in with them. She waved at them, which made him wonder if they knew each other or just in passing. This was her territory, her playground. He felt truly out of place, as they reached a stop sign, one of the young kid revving his green Harley up. She flipped him off, which earned a hearty laugh from the man. He breathed a sigh of relief, thankful that nothing bad would happen.

"You up for a race sweet cheeks?!" Came the voice to the left. A heavily tatted man, with a Mohawk on his head. He gritted his teeth, hoping she would decline. He could feel, under his fingers that she was itching for one. He was in her fate and frankly he wasn't sure if he wanted to be a part of it right at this second.

"I'm taking a rain check, Razor. Gotta take this old geezer home." She said, over the roar of the engines. Which earned a hearty laugh from all the men that surrounded them. The man clapped her on the shoulder, which earned him a punch in the shoulder. He definitely was out of his territory.

"Well when you head back. Me, Trick, and young buck on your right will be waiting. You got some mad skills." Razor said to her, as he made a signal at the others around him. "Head out guys!" He yelled, the roar of different breeds of motorcycles roaring as they all headed out. He could sense the obvious disappointment as her shoulders dropped, but it was gone in a heartbeat, as she roared hers loudly, placed her helmet back on her head, taking off fast and hard. His fingers slipped a little, not ready for the hasty take off, but recovered quickly as she headed off into the direction the arrow had on the GPS.

The ride back seemed longer, as they made their way back to the outskirts of the city. He wondered if she'd go back to the city, where all those guys were at, or go back to her apartment. The sun was bright and glaring into his eyes. He had never thought, when they first ventured out this morning, they'd be out this long. Sure, he enjoyed himself, but the vibrations of the bike made him feel like he had a permanent erection. Not that he minded the feeling, but he needed his release and soon. But he had business to attend to first, as they got closer to his home, several of the men waiting outside for his return. He chuckled, as he noticed Charles wave like a child who hadn't seen their friend in forever. It was a bit annoying to at the same time, but amusing at the same time. It was then, as the bike stopped in his drive, that he had never felt so much freedom in a while. The rush, the adrenaline, felt amazing to him. But he wasn't going to make a habit of it, at least not often anyways.

"You can come inside, if you want." He told her, after he took the helmet off. The wind sweeping over his face, as he breathed in the smell of the air around him. He hadn't done that since earlier, as he handed her the helmet to him. She shook her head, as she lifted the lid up on her. A small smile playing on her face.

"Not today. I'm famished and I've kept you long enough." She said with a chuckle, as she revved her engine as her way of showing off for him, or for the whole lot of them. He wasn't sure, but it earned a round of applause from several of the men. "I'll see you tomorrow. Keep the helmet." She said as they kissed briefly. He ran a thumb over her bottom lip, as their eyes locked. He wondered why she seemed hesitant now, he wanted to question her about it, but she shook her head a bit, as she put the flap down. He watched as she backed out of the drive, revved the engine once more, before peeling out leaving a cloud of smoke behind her. He shook his head, as he turned around looking at the men before him; instant business mode turning on for him.

"Be in my office in twenty." He told them all, walking into the house, as he immediately went to his bedroom to take a shower. He smelt like rain water, dirt, and whatever else that they had traveled through that day. His hair was a sweat rag, and as he stood under the spray of the scorching hot water, he wondered what had happened in those final moments. Why had she seemed so sad, even though the smile had reached her eyes, or maybe it was just to make him feel at ease? He sighed, as he washed his body and hair, feeling his tense muscles relax under the hot spray of the water. He got out of the shower, towel dried himself off before putting some casual clothes on. He knew they'd probably ask what had happened between him and Emily, but it wasn't any of their business really.

He walked into his room, noticing all of his things; that had been in his pockets, were on the bed. He smiled, knowing that his house maid had been here to gather his clothes from last night. He put his phone on the charger, that was next to the nightstand, before walking out of the room and headed to his study. A few of the guys were chatting, some were sitting down with their legs propped up, but once he cleared his throat they immediately stopped what they were doing and stood to their feet. He walked over to the ones that had been sitting a few moments previously, glaring at them.

"I don't pay you guys to be lazy fuckers. If I see either of you doing that again, your ass will be fired, and David won't be your saving grace. Understood?" He asked them, looking the two men square in the eye, which caused a chuckle from behind him. He turned to the sound, noticing it happened to be the punk kid Charles. He gritted his teeth, as he stood in front of him. "You are fired. I'm tired of your childish antics. Out. Now." He said staring him straight in the eyes, finally doing what he should have done from the start. The young kid looked at David, but his head of security nodded his head towards the door. He walked over to his desk, sitting down on the edge of it. "You have the floor, D." He finally said after a long silence. He was waiting for someone to speak out of line, but they all seem too intimated. He knew they were when he turned into business form. His only hope was that this meeting wouldn't take too long, because he knew he had some things to catch up on before tomorrow morning.

"Thanks, S." David said to him, with a brief nod as he stood in front of the guys. He noticed a few had taken out a notepad, and a pencil. While others hadn't. He walked around his desk, as his HOS started to talk about last night, and sat down in his chair. He listened to the whole spiel about how Isabelle tried to threaten his empire, and that his lawyers were once again involved in the matter. He sighed, rubbing his forehead, as he heard the news. This was something he had *hoped* wouldn't happen again. He thought to himself, as he opened a drawer, which had the previous case about him and the sorry excuse of a woman. He knew David had a copy, especially when he was telling the men bits and pieces of what went down then and there. One guy muttered bitch under his breathe, which he chuckled at, but didn't say anything else. What was Isabelle try playing at? He wondered, as he rubbed his scratchy face, as he tuned out the meeting and looked through the old file once again.

Once the meeting had been over, he shook his head at David; not wanting to talk about what had gone on, when the man had lingered back to have a word with him. The other man just nodded his head, before closing the door behind him. He rubbed his face once more, as he turned on some music, putting it on shuffle from his iPod dock, and the song *Crawling into The Dark* by Hoobastank started to play. He let the lyrics and music consume him for a moment, before he turned on his computer and wondered if she had made it home safely. He texted her, and the only response was a 'yep.' He frowned at the response, but figured she was busy eating and doing what she did before she turned in for the night. His mind drifted to the night before, giving him an instant hard on. He wanted to go over there, bring her here and get lost inside of her, but he couldn't let things get to far behind or he drown in all the things that needed his attention. He sighed, as he opened the first email, of many, and got to work.

CHAPTER 15

THE DAYS SEEMED TO become routine for her, the nights seemed longer as her old demons started to haunt her once more. She had tried to avoid him, but that hadn't worked, especially when they worked in the same building. But the whole him being wealthy, having an empire of his own, was a bit overwhelming. Sure, they had a great time going to different places, but she felt ultimately that she was slowing him down. It had been an amazing month together, but the old demons she feared were coming back. She was nervous, worried, and unsure of the whole relationship. The words of Mark, even Ethan had constantly played in the back of her mind *you ain't shit and won't ever get a great man.* And now that she did, she felt as if, at any day, those words would come true again. Everything seemed too good to be true, it was a bit unnerving. Even though the day that Sean had announced that she'd have Conner, as her own personal security, had almost been a deal breaker until he had reminded her why it was necessary. She didn't like it, still didn't, but at least he didn't hover around her. She thought with a sigh.

She looked out at the night sky before her, through her apartment window, as she did almost every other night now, sometimes even when she knew he was asleep at his place she'd do the same. His place had been overwhelming at first, especially when everything so fresh, so clean, and yet felt like a fragile being all in the same. She had been uncomfortable with the tour of the whole place; a two story condo with at least five bedrooms. His being on the bottom floor, with his study nearby. It was all done in a Victorian feel, but still every time she stepped inside of his home, she felt like she had to be on her best behavior and it drove her mad. It had led to some mind blowing sex however, especially when he had tied her up and used the shackle bar on her. She never thought he was into that scene, but he had proven her wrong time and again. The thought brought a smile to her face, as she remembered just a few days ago he had shown her something new. Neither one played the sub role well, which had been determined the first day.

She waited for him by the door, as he had just walked by the staircase to warn the guys to not bother them for a few hours. The thought made her giggle, as he came back with a smirk on his face. She knew the guys had given him hell, they always managed to do so. He opened the door for her, and she stepped in. The room was automatically lit up by the sensor lights, which she figured had been installed years ago. It was the only room of the house that had a modern day look. Nothing medieval or Victorian style about it at all. She walked over to the riding horse, something that hadn't been here before. He had promised they try something new, and by the looks of it this had to do with anal sex.

"So you want to claim my ass, mister?" She asked with a sarcastic undertone in her voice. It wasn't the first time he had, but she knew the fundamentals of it. He chuckled as he came over to her, giving her a brief kiss on the lips. They always seemed to up the ante on one another here. They knew the rules, and stuck by them.

"Who's to say I haven't already, madam?" He replied with a wink, causing her to giggle. She always seemed to be giggling around him, no matter what was going on. But resumed her stoic poise when he started to undress her. It was a battle of who'd play the top dog in here, but in the end of the day they always managed to wing it. They both were switches, but neither wanted to admit it.

She smiled at the memory, it was a beautiful one, even if her ass had been sore for several days later. To say she wasn't able to sit for several days, was an understatement. People had asked her, at work, why she hadn't been able to sit for too long. And the only reason was she had sunburned her ass while in the tanning bed. Of course that story had wound its way around the whole building, to Sean himself. He had gloated about that ever since, that was under she had threatened to castrate him if he continued. Needless to say that shut him up real quick. She turned her head however, when she heard her phone vibrate on the night stand. It was near morning, from the way the sky looked. Another night had gone without sleep, it was becoming a natural thing for her, as she picked up the phone seeing it was a long distance call. Frowning at the number, she declined it, hoping whoever it was would just leave a voicemail, but there wasn't one after she waited several minutes for one to pop up.

She went to take a shower, her thoughts a jumbled mess, as she wondered if she was truly enough for Sean. She was a wild child, who embraced risking everything for the thrill. The last time she had raced on her motorcycle, against Razor and his group of guys, she thought she had given him a coronary at first. It was his idea to tag along that day. Never did she imagine ever being yelled at, for her *almost* crash. Sure, her dad had gone off on her for her dangerous habits, but all the men of her past had embraced it. Maybe that was another reason she felt like she wasn't enough for the man. That they were both dragging each other down somehow, as she stood under the hot scolding spray of the shower. At least that's how she felt, as she got out of the shower and towel dried herself off, before going to her closet to pick out an outfit for the day. She saw the Elizabeth and James Black Eri Strapless Wide-Leg Jumpsuit, near the front. She hadn't worn it yet, and decided to do so. Maybe he would get a heart attack over this little number, especially when her tattoos were noticeable. She had gotten a few new ones, a few more birds that were now on her shoulders. They were all flying down to the flowers that were in the middle of her back. No one, not even her body guard, knew she had left her building during the middle of the night to do it, a few days ago. She loved it, and as she put her Black Louboutin Milleo Suede Lattice Red Sole Pumps on her feet and grabbed her things to head out, she wondered if he'd get pissed if he found out. Laughing to herself, she shrugged, not really caring at the moment.

She walked to the front of the building, seeing Conner had already opened the door for her. One of the perks of being the boss' girlfriend, but at the same time annoyed her to the max. He closed the door, once she got inside the vehicle, and waited for him to drive her off to her place of work. She noticed he was shaking his head, which peaked her interest, as they headed out onto the packed streets of the city.

"Mind telling what's on your mind, C?" She asked him, after she had put some Chapstick on her lips. The man chuckled and looked at her through the rear view mirror as if she didn't already know.

"Other than you getting new tats and wearing a revealing outfit..."

"Revealing? Hah! The only thing this shows is my tattoos, not my breasts or my coochy. So hush your mouth, Conner Dillweed." She said in a defensive tone, as she flipped him the bird. He laughed even more, but stopped when he noticed the look she was giving him. The rest of the ride was in silence, and when he pulled up to the building she got out without a second glance back. She walked inside, heading straight for the elevators. She wasn't going to be treated like a child, and it seemed like ever since she had gotten close to another wreck, a few weeks past, Sean had wanted to keep a close eye on here without trying to be noticeable about it. She wasn't going to have it. She pressed the top floor button, tapping her heeled foot impatiently as the door closed and slowly climbed up.

Once the doors opened, she immediately fast paced her way to his office, ignoring the calls for his personal assistants; she still believed they were ditzy fucks, even more so now that she was up here every so often. She opened the door, seeing the man himself hanging up the phone and loosening the tie he had on at the same time. She could tell he was pissed, as he looked up at her, as she walked over to him their eyes locked on the entire time.

"You need to..."

"If you fucking tell me I need to watch my mouth, in front of cheese head again. Forget it. I'm not..."

R. A. B.

"I don't want you to…"

"What? Get hurt? End up in the hospital again? Die like…"

"God damnit Emily Night! Do you even give a flying fuck about your safety?! Let alone…" He stopped talking mid-sentence as she started to laugh. This fool couldn't be serious right? She thought to herself, which made her laugh that much harder till her sides hurt, until she completely stopped and glared at him, as she stepped closer to him. They were nose to nose, eye to eye.

"You aren't going to tell me how to run my life, Sean. Ever since that race, where I *almost* crashed at, you've been…" She paused, closed her eyes briefly, before looking him dead in the eyes. "Suffocating. It's as if…"

"What Emily? As if what?" He asked her, after she hadn't said anything for several minutes. A lone tear escaped from her eyes, and she stepped back. It wasn't worth getting into right now. She fixed his tie, kissed him on the lips, not wanting to take it much more than that. But it seemed as if he wanted to. She melted into the kiss, as she wrapped her arms around his neck. A slow sensual kiss that held so much meaning, without resolving much of anything.

"I have to go. I don't want…"

"Your with me, they'll…"

"No I want to keep my good reputation of an excellent worker." She told him, rubbing off the lip chap she had on, off of his lips. He sighed, as she squeezed his hand briefly.

"Why do I feel like you're walking away?" He asked, after she started to head towards the door. She knew he could see the newest additions to her back, but either he was to focused on them to say much, or didn't want to pick another fight with her. Either way she turned towards him, with her hand on the doorknob and gave him a sweet little smile.

"Only to work." She said, opening the door and headed down the hallway, ignoring both of the girls at the desk, to get to the elevator. She wasn't going to keep dealing with being treated like a child. If he wanted to mold her into something she wasn't, she'd drop his ass in a heartbeat. The door pinged open, she stepped inside and pressed the number for her floor, as she heard him calling her name with a roar. She flipped him off just as the doors closed and she headed down to her floor to work. She didn't want him to intervene with her career, which she was glad he hadn't, but she sure as hell wasn't going to be treated like a child either. The doors pinged open, and she headed straight for her office, ignoring the wolf whistles from several of the men; who had been trying to get in her pants for a few weeks now.

She turned on the lights in the small room, noticing the paper work already on her desk. The head of this floor thought mighty high of her, maybe because she had proved her worth time and time again. Most of the others slacked off, and didn't get as many clients as she did, which from what she had been told was a record high for the company. To say she didn't celebrate, the day she had heard about this fact was an understatement. Turning on the laptop, as she sat down in her chair, she noticed that one of the men were standing in her doorway, hesitant to come in. She got back up, and closed the door in his face. Today wasn't the day for creepy stalkers, she was pissed off enough as it was, without anymore unnecessary drama to happen. She picked up a sheet of paper up and set to work, but also thought of that particular day.

Hearing the news had been music to her ears. She was itching for the end of the day to get here. It had only been several weeks, several weeks since she had come to the New York division but was already getting high praises for her work. It was such an amazing feeling, as she watched the time tick on and finally hit five pm. She turned off her laptop, grabbed her purse, before heading out of her office, as she headed out for the day. Several of the men were all in a group talking about something. She waved at them, as she went to the elevators. They pinged open and she headed down. Not even bothering to head to the top floor. She wanted to get drunk, hell it was the end of the week anyways!

She got off at the garage level, got into her new vehicle; a Jaguar convertible. She didn't love it as much as her other two, but it was a beauty and that was all that mattered. She started the engine, it purred to life, as she sped out of the parking garage and headed for a liquor store. Once she purchased her alcohol she went back to her apartment. She took her flats off the moment she got in, opened one of the bottles of Jack and the rest was history.

She chuckled at the memory, especially when she had been so ridiculously drunk that she had no clue she had called Sean, till the next morning when she had a terrible hangover. She had never seen him so pissed off, till the following weekend where she had almost gotten into a wreck with her Yamaha. That had been a very long ride back home, and the thought of it just pissed her off more. It all came back down to the feeling that she was dragging him down, and the thought was unsettling, but at the same time she felt it were the truth. She rubbed her forehead as she began to work on the things that needed to be done.

The day went on, and she had finished her work early. She had been avoiding all of his phone calls and texts, throughout the day. She had no desire to get into another argument, especially after the day she had. Licking her chapped lips, downing the coffee that her bodyguard had picked up for her not to long ago, she turned off the laptop and was happy about how productive today had been. Turning off the lights to her office, she headed to the elevators, pressing the down button. There was no use going to the top floor, when she knew he usually worked late anyways. As the doors opened to the lobby area, she decided then and there to walk home. It looked nice outside, so she didn't mind doing just that, as she waved off Conner at the entrance, put her headphones in her ears, and walked to her apartment building.

CHAPTER 16

IT HAD BEEN A great past month for them both, even though they had a few mishaps in between. He had been a nervous wreck every time she had decided to get on her motorcycle, especially after she had almost wrecked into a pole a few weeks ago. But even so, he had noticed the slight change in her attitude towards him. As if she was pulling away from him, but was trying to hide the fact that she was. It was confusing to him, making him wonder what he had done wrong but his mind drew a blank at the whole thing, even though he noticed that she had been more rebellious than usual. That was something that also bothered him. The fact of the matter was, he was starting to fall in love with her, nothing like it had been with Isabelle but this was different. And if the conversation that he just had with Emily, though be it brief with her flipping him off as the doors to the elevator closed, he had seen the true her. He had seen the girl behind the brave face, behind the sassy and smart remarks, that she was scared. Scared of what he wasn't sure, but he would get to the bottom of it, after he found out the answer to when she got the new tats. He sighed as he rubbed his face, walking back to his office, both women looking at him dumbfounded and lost as he went inside his office.

He sat down at his desk, putting his head into hands, hoping this wouldn't be another long day of her avoiding him, but even so he knew how that worked out. If she didn't like being treated like a child as she put it, she'd do anything in her power to ignore him.

R. A. B.

It happened several times in the past few weeks, especially after the wreck she had almost gotten into with the biker guys. They all seemed like great guys, though he had always been hesitant to speak to any of them, he always felt like he'd get beat up if he said or did the wrong thing. He sighed, as he got a text from Conner telling him that she had flipped him off this morning. He chuckled, at least he hadn't been the only one today. His thoughts went back to the time where he had asked her to move in with him, which ended up with a sort of half answer, but even so he wasn't even sure if there had been a real answer to begin with.

She was laughing. Laughing at the fact he had just asked her to move in with him. He wasn't sure what was so funny, sure they hadn't been together for long, but he felt like they could last. Last forever if not until one of them died. Which he hoped wouldn't happen anytime soon. He lay there, naked in his bed, with her laying on her back. The nipple clamps still attached to her breasts. He hadn't bothered to take them off when he asked her the off handed question. Maybe that was why she laughed? He thought to himself, as he undid the clamps causing her to moan from the effects of it. He smirked, as his hand trailed down her chest to her stomach, then to her pussy, as he could feel how wet she was for him with only a slight touch. Always ready. Always willing to play.

"Answer me." He said in a seductive like tone, as he started to finger her core center, the soft moans escaping from the woman that lay next to him, as he lazily swirled his tongue around her nipples. He heard her hiss with pleasure, but said nothing more than that.

"God. Don't. Stop." She said through her clenched teeth as he put another finger inside of her, pumping her faster as he sucked hard on her right breast that was nearest to him. She moaned, writhing beneath him as he could feel her getting close to yet another orgasm. He had lost count of how many she had had that night, but he enjoyed every minute of it as she got on top of him. He took his fingers out of her and the rest of was history.

The memory made him hard in an instant, but knew that he needed to control himself because of all the meetings he had this morning.

124

One being with his lawyer then God knows what else after. He sighed, as he thought maybe he should ask again but wasn't sure when, especially when he wanted to get to the bottom of what was really bothering her. He just hoped it wasn't to major, or bad, but he was worried about her. Very worried. He had noticed the dark circles under her eyes, when she didn't think he paid that close attention to her. She was always a lively person but the fact of the matter was something was wrong. The lone tear, he saw not too long ago made him see a glimpse of it. He sighed, as he twirled the pen in his fingers before calling her. No answer. It was going to be one of those days he thought shaking his head just thinking about it.

The meetings he had seemed to drag on forever that day, his mind preoccupied with thoughts of her. He hid his obvious worry, in front of his fellow colleagues but when it was over he thought about her. David had mentioned something about her going to the cafeteria earlier with a spaced out look. He didn't ask much more, but he did dig deep into her personal history. Something he hated doing but when he saw that she suffered from insomnia and depression, he knew he needed to bring her back to the light. She was his night in a storm clouded with wrong thoughts, he'd have to bring her back into the light. And even though he wanted to get her father involved, whom it seemed she had always been close to from the exclusive background check, he knew it wouldn't be a good decision. At least for now.

He felt around the bed, noticing the chill next to him. He frowned, as he immediately woke up, seeing her near the window looking out at the view. She was wearing his shirt, her hand swiped a stray hair out of her face. He took the covers off of him, as he walked over to her, putting his arms around her once he reached her.

"Everything okay?" He asked, the worry evident in his voice. She leaned back into his chest, sighing contently.

"Yeah." She said to him, he kissed the top of her forehead as they stood there for a few minutes in a comfortable silence. His worry about her being up at this time of night, went to the back of his mind.

He rubbed his face, remembering that night like it was only yesterday, when it happened only a week ago. He looked at the clock in the wall, noticing it was a little after five. The day had flown by like it always did. A knock interrupted his thoughts, he looked up noticing it was both David and Conner. Usually it wasn't either one, but Emily. He scratched his face, feeling the stubble there. He immediately knew that it had to do with her, if they both seemed unsure of who should speak first. He leaned back in his chair, with his leg crossed over his other and waited.

"Speak up or walk out." He finally said, after neither one of them had said anything. He knew he sounded annoyed, but he didn't feel like playing games right now. Unless they went to a casino, which he had no use for to begin with, seeing as he had enough money to last him for years to come anyways. He was never particularly fond of them even before his status of billionaire came along.

"It's about Emily." Conner said as he stepped over to him. He got up from his seat instantly. Had she been hurt? Or worse in the hospital? He hoped it wasn't that, he wasn't sure if he could take such news.

"She walked home...."

"She what Dill weed?! You just...."

"You know how frightening she can..."

"I don't let her temper get the best of me, Conner! Did you even bother to follow her home? Or did..."

"She texted me that..."

"Texted you?! The nerve of the woman! Let's go!" He yelled, grabbing the young man's shirt. He didn't have to tell David what to do, he saw him go to his desk to grab the work that he would look over later. He headed out the door, with Conner in front. He didn't say a single word to either woman, they knew he wasn't in the mood just from the scene before them. He got to the elevator, pressed the down button and got in after the doors pinged open. He shoved the man in, and the doors closed behind them. He let go of his shirt, crossed his arms but said nothing else. The young man opened and closed his mouth before saying nothing. It was probably better he didn't. He thought to himself, as the doors opened up several more times before they got to the garage level floor. He immediately walked to Lamborghini and got in. He hadn't had her out in a while, and thought it was a good day to do it. He gritted his teeth, as he watched the two men get into the other vehicle before he sped off out onto the busy streets of the city. He needed to get to her. He needed to figure out what was wrong before it was too late to help. He just hoped that she'd let him inside, not her apartment but her feelings. Hell, he had a damn key to the place thanks to her. He thought with a smirk on his face.

He got to the apartment building, parking a row over to the now growing collection of sports cars. He shook his head, as he got out of his car, and saw another new motorcycle next to the Yamaha; a Harley. He ran a finger over the metallic body of the new addition, as it shinned brightly in the fading light of the day, before he headed to the elevator and pressed the up button. The doors opened and he pressed the number for her floor. It seemed to take forever, when really it took only a few seconds and he was on the floor. Walking down the hallway, he heard; laughter, yelling, more laughter among other things. He chuckled when he noticed the familiar sounds of someone having sex, obviously they didn't care how loud they were, till he finally reached her place. Knocking on the door seemed better than just.... barging in, even if he had the key to the place. He knocked, several times before the door opened just enough for her petite body to show through.

"Sean. What are you doing here?" She asked in a surprised voice. He placed a hand on her door, opening wider for him to come inside. She didn't stop him, so that was a good thing in his book. He came inside, closing the door behind him.

"Well it seems you gave Conner the slip and..."

"Do you think I give a fuck about..."

"Drop the act, Em." He said as he stepped closer to her, inhaling her familiar scent that he loved so much. She looked at him confused, as he ran a hand down her face and over her bottom lip. He kissed her gently on the lips, before holding her close to him. He could sense the hesitation. Why he never felt it before was beyond him. Was she scared of him? Scared of what they were? He sighed inwardly wishing she wasn't going through such turmoil inside. Had she had that bad of relationships in the past to make her feel like she had always had to be brave? He wondered to himself, as he kissed the top of her forehead.

"What act?" She said as she looked him into his eyes; blue to hazel. He wiped a stray hair off of her face, searching her eyes for any sorts of clues. But he found nothing. Maybe that is why he hadn't noticed the signs before now? He wasn't sure, but he he'd find out the truth soon! He sighed inwardly as he took her hand, walking to the bedroom, set her down on it before pacing back and forth. He could feel her eyes on him the entire time.

"The one where you have to act tough for..."

"Act tough? What are you..."

"Emily don't act like you don't..."

"Look Sean, how dare you *insinuate* how I feel? Let alone how I think?" She asked, getting up off of the bed and jabbing her finger into his chest. He said nothing as he took her hand and kissed the center of it. She glared at him before removing her hand from his grasp. He stepped closer to her, so there was no space left. Her hands immediately going for his tie, but he put his hands on top of hers shaking his head slightly.

"I'm worried about you. I just..."

"Worried about me? Boss you have nothing..."

"You hardly ever call me boss. Why won't..."

"Look I just…" She paused, taking a step back from him. He tried to reach for her, but she seemed to shut him out. He rubbed his face, looking at her with a puzzled expression. She had never seemed this shut out before. Maybe it was deeper than meets the eye. He watched as she walked over to the window, letting some of the light from the streets come into the room. The sky was a beautiful shade of colors, as the sun set down for the day. "I can't be what you want, Sean. I'm like my last name. Dark and deadly as the night itself. Can't you see it?" She said in a mere whisper. It was so low that he wasn't sure if he had heard things or not. But he knew he did. He had definitely heard it.

"Emily that's not true. I want you…"

"No. No you don't." Her voice sounded weak, defeated even. It hurt him just hearing her say that about herself. He walked over to her, placing his arms around her waist. The obvious tear tracks were falling silently onto her oversized shirt.

"Why would you say that my darling sweet girl?" He whispered to her, as he brushed some of the red locks from her face. In the time that he had known her, she had cut her hair in a small wavish looking bob thing, but now it was starting to get longer. He liked it this length, especially when he pulled it during sex. He immediately crossed that thought out of his head, as he held onto her. He didn't know how long they stayed in the silence of the room, looking out at the city before them, but he needed her to understand. He wanted her to realize he wasn't going to be the rest of those other guys she had been with. Ever.

"You say you want me now, Sean. But what about when you get bored of my spunky attitude or…"

"That won't happen. You keep me on my toes enough as it is to ever get bored of you." He told her, which earned him a jab in the ribs and a giggle all at the same time. He smirked, as he turned her around, wiping the tears off of her face. He could see the scared little girl now, the one that seemed to put on a brave face for everyone, but just as quickly as it was there it was gone just like that. They both turned as the sound of his phone ringing, he took it out of his pocket noticing it was only Conner trying to reach him. He was about to press the ignore button, when she snatched it out of his hand and accepted it for him, but placed it on speakerphone.

"Look dilly whacker me and the big B are fucking like horny rabbits. Do you mind calling back when it's semi important?!" She exclaimed dramatically over the phone. He could hear the obvious laughter in the background, and knew the younger man was probably beet red now at the same time. Nevertheless it was funny just thinking about it. He just hoped that David was around to set him straight.

"Oh um… I'm sorry to bother you…"

"You dipshit she was teasing you." Came the voice of David, causing them both to laugh hysterically by the choice of words his HOS used. He had a feeling they were only checking in to see how things were going, but he definitely wasn't going to discuss it over the phone, with her standing right beside him. Maybe in private if they ever finished the conversation, but by the looks of things it probably wasn't going to happen. He watched as she headed over to the bed, laid down on it, and patted the side next her. He raised an eyebrow at her, shaking his head briefly, which ended up making him catch a pillow that had been thrown at him as a response.

"Look I'll get back to you guys later, and David keep a close eye on Conner just in case he goes off on a search for the next available thing with two legs." He said back, which earned not only a giggle from Emily, but a growl from the other end of the telephone, before hanging up. Chuckling, he set the phone on the small table nearest the window, before walking over to the bed, leaning over it as he kissed her hard on the lips, as she pulled him down onto the bed, him beneath her. Smirking up her, he ran a hand to her thigh, causing a small shiver to course through her body, before resting both of his hands onto her hips. He wanted to continue the conversation but it seemed as she wanted to play, not that he minded or anything but he didn't want to damper the mood either. He rolled them over, so that he pinned her down under him. Her foot raised up, as she rubbed his erection that was slowly forming in his pants. He wanted to take the oversized shirt off of her, it had been one of his till she had claimed it. It looked better on her anyways.

"What's so amusing?" She asked him, after she had rolled them over and sat down on top of him, before undoing his tie till it was on with side of his jacket. He ran his fingers up and down her arm, before wrapping his arms around her until he was in a sitting position. The tie was now in his hands, after pulling it roughly from its place; never once taking his eyes off of her. He could see the amusement in her eyes, as he put it around her neck but didn't tie it into a knot.

"You wearing my clothes amuses me." He said in a seductive tone, as he pulled her closer to him, with the ends capturing her lips with his. He could feel her smile against him, before the kiss became passionate and desperate. It was as if she was trying to pour all of her soul into it, which just made him want all of her then and now. He rolled her onto her back, breaking the kiss as he took the oversized shirt off of her tiny frame, throwing it behind him.

"I thought I kept you on your toes, Sean. Or is..."

"You do that as well." He said to her, as he kissed his way down her body, before ripping her panties off of her. "Hope you didn't like those." He teased her, looking up at her from where he was at.

"Not at all." She replied sarcastically, before letting out a hiss as he flicked her clit with one of his fingers, before using his tongue to work his usual magic. He blew gently as he felt her hands grip onto his hair, as he; lapped, suck and gently nipped at her pussy. He always noticed after several times of going slow, then going as fast as he possibly could, that she was getting close to orgasm. It was the way she screamed for him to go faster, the way she called his name, and putting his face that much closer that he had no choice but to go faster. He loved it though, hearing her come undone as he unleashed his tongue around her folds, and then also her clit. His dick was rock hard, and with his free hand; he was using his fingers on the other to guide her that much closer to the edge, to jack himself off. The ache to be inside of her was overwhelming, as he dived his tongue lapping up the juices, before the actual storm would hit.

He could tell she was holding back, it wasn't the first time, so he made a few noise against her clit, and that's when it happened. The organs ricocheted through her, as he swallowed the cum that came out dry. The moment he knew she was done, he laid down next to her, allowing her a few moments to come down from her own high. But it seemed that wasn't on her mind, as she flipped him onto his back, tying his hands to each of the bedposts, with a string she had somehow had next to the bed. He smirked knowing he had done that a few weeks back, which caused her to giggle when he had done it. It definitely wouldn't be the last time this would happen either, as he heard the telltale sign of the dresser drawer opening and the condom packet being ripped open to produce the condom out of it. She sat on his legs, putting it on his hardened member.

He watched her sit on top of him, place her hands on his chest as leverage, before slowly going up and down on him. He noticed she hadn't tied the strings that tight though, since he could flex his wrists around. He had a feeling she did that on purpose, but for the sole purpose of letting her have control for now, he acted like he didn't notice. His thoughts were becoming scrambled, as she went faster, using the posts for leeway, before orgasming once more. He smirked devilishly as he got his hands out of the strings, before flipping her around so he was back on top. He pounded inside of her, calling her name into the darkening room of night. The sounds of outside were tuned out, as he fucked her good and well into the night.

CHAPTER 17

YELLOW WAS ALL SHE could see as she came to, the next morning. She placed her hand on the side of her bed noticing the chill there. She bolted upright, as the glare from the sun seemed to be more pronounced than usual, before looking at the time on the clock next to her bed. It was well past eight, it had been almost one in the afternoon even, and she was late for work. Very late she thought, cursing at the fact her alarm hadn't gone off in time. But what confused her was why Sean wasn't there, nor was any of the clothes he had on from yesterday either. She gritted her teeth, as un-welcomed thoughts came to her mind. One being he had left without even so much as a goodbye and the other being he had just said those things to her last night to get inside of her pants. She pushed the thoughts away, before putting some casual and immediately grabbed her things before walking into the living room to see if she had anything that needed to be taken with her to work.

She just hoped she wouldn't get fired, she had never been *this* late in her life, and she didn't like the feeling of being rushed either. Even when she lived at home, she hated when her father had woken her up early to rush her out of the house to get to school or work. There was always an argument that followed, but that was beside the point. She put on her shoes, seeing as she didn't bother getting to dressed up; it would've just taken that much longer to get to work. She groaned, hoping her boss would give her a chance to explain, as she grabbed her keys for her Harley and headed to the elevators, after making sure her apartment door was locked. Once she got to the ground level garage, she hopped onto her Harley, revving up the engine to let some of her anger show through and rode off onto the busy streets. Weaving in and out of traffic, she finally made it to her job, and made her way to the elevators to get to her floor.

The doors opened, and she noticed that everyone was busy doing their normal thing as she headed to Kelly's office. His door was closed, the light off, sighing heavily she made it to her office turning on the lights to get to work. Setting her things down, she noticed the work she had to get done. The only thing she had forgotten to bring with her, was her phone, but at the moment she didn't care as she set to work. It was going to take her well into after closing hours to get all this done and dealt with. Her mind went to Sean, questioning why he had left without waking her, and why her alarm had been shut off. She had noticed a piece of paper, by her lamp but hadn't bothered to pick it up or read it. And if she had, maybe then that would've explained. Shrugging it didn't matter right now.

A knock sounded on her door, not too long after she had got well into editing someone's novel. It was a really good, minus a few certain things in it, as she looked up to see it was her boss Mr. Kelly standing at the door. She stood up, brushing off the pencil shavings from her shirt, and ushered him in; closing the door behind them. The older man took her seat, causing her to take the ones usually held for clients. Her palms started to sweat as she felt nervous of what he would say to her. A gentle smile played on his face, which confused her but she didn't show it on her face. Did Sean have something to do with her sleeping this late? She wondered, even though she had felt refreshed and her body felt relaxed from their late night fuck session, but that didn't excuse him either. She had a job to do, and being late for whatever noble reason he had, wasn't right in her book.

"Miss Night no need to worry. I had been under the assumption you wouldn't be in today." He said with a gently tone, which earned him a raised eyebrow. What had Sean done? She didn't like how this was going. Her boss' tone wasn't in the highest regards, or at least that is what she read from it anyways. Her guard was now up.

"I don't understand, sir. I usually have my alarm set, but for some reason it didn't go off this morning. I do apologize." She said to him, hoping he'd believe her, and not think it was some excuse. Hell, she'd be damned if she got fired for this! She thought to herself, as she picked at a string on her jeans. Maybe she should've just went to *him* instead and chewed him out. After all, it was his fault that she had been very late to work. She gritted her teeth, as the sudden urge to hit him came over her.

"Well I don't condone my employees to be late. Neither does Mr. Bowling himself, but you are a great worker. The best I've seen in a long time, but if this happens again I will coach you or fire you. Let this be a warning, ma'am. I don't give warnings often either. And you will be staying late tonight as well." He said to her, raising up from the chair, before walking over to her. They shook hands before he left her to it. A million thoughts running through her head, one being had he even told people about them? Or was she just some secret for him to be there at night for? She ran a hand through her red locks, knowing she needed to get it cut again. She sat down in the chair, with a heavy thump, and set to work. Oh how she wished she had just stayed home, even now that she had to stay late after hours, not that she wasn't going to already but hearing it from her boss just made it seem like a punishment for her lateness. She booted up the computer, as she continued to edit the manuscript that she had been reading before her boss came into her office, to give her the warning. She sighed inwardly, as she signed onto the computer once it had finally booted up. She wanted to talk to Sean himself, get the answers as to why he left without telling her and why he had turned her alarm off, but she wasn't going to bother him. Her anger was getting to her, and she didn't feel like exploding on someone who *cared* about her.

The hours ticked by though, but she had gotten a lot of the work done. Slacking off wasn't in her book, as she came back from the cafeteria with some food in a bag. She had been in such a rush earlier, that she had forgotten to pack anything up. Putting her hair in a loose ponytail, she stepped inside of her office, stopping in her tracks as she did so. The CEO himself was leaning against her desk, a playful smile on his face. She glared at him, sat down in her chair, ignoring him as she took a bite from her turkey sandwich. He cleared his throat, as she heard the door click shut and the blinds be drawn close. She huffed in frustration, finally looking up at him.

"What the fuck do you want, Mr. Bowling?" She said through gritted teeth, as she clenched her fists together. Seeing him now, in his own domain, after hours of wondering why he left without a single word this more, brought the anger and hurt to the surface tenfold. Her thoughts playing its usual tricks on her, but she refused to listen to them at the moment. He walked over to her, sitting on the desk as he clasped his fingers together.

"Don't take that tone..."

"Tone?! How dare you tell me, don't take that tone with you, Sean. You. Made. Me. Late. Today!" She said jabbing him into the chest, between each word, after she had gotten up from her chair. He took her hand, the ever present spark of electricity was there, but she took her hand out of his grasp before punching him in the jaw. He looked at her, with amazement in his eyes, as if he couldn't believe she had done that.

"Why did you just hit me Emily? Did you get my message? Or did..."

"What message? You left, you fucking left me this morning. You promised to..."

"I wanted you to take..."

"Wanted me to take the day off? Wanted me to catch up on fucking sleep?! You have no fucking right to assume I needed the day off!" She said wanting to strike him again, but wasn't sure if she was taking it too far or not, but did it really matter. He was smirking as if it was not big deal. Growling she hit him again, this time in the shoulder, but he didn't flinch. It was as if he was letting her do this. She stepped away from him, walked to the door, and opened it up for him. She didn't have time to play some childish stupid game.

"Is that what you want? Me to leave?" He asked her calmly, as if this was a normal every day conversation. She looked at him, wondering what he was playing at but said nothing. What more did they need to say to each other? Especially when she felt like she was going to go off even more at him.

"I have nothing else to say to you. Have a..."

"You're breaking up..."

"Don't put words in my mouth that I didn't say. Just go." She said to him, not wanting to deal with this right now. Maybe later, she just didn't want to mess with this right now. He walked over to her, leaned over to kiss her but she turned her head away instead. He left the office, but she didn't bother watching him leave. She looked at the people who had been watching the scene unfold. Or what was left of it anyways, but they knew better to ask her questions. It really wasn't any of their business, but she had a feeling the rumor mill would be in full force within the hour or less. Closing the door behind her, she sat down to eat her food. Her thoughts on what the note had consisted of, but figured it wasn't important anymore since she was here, and got back to work.

She knew it was going home time, a few hours later, as she heard the chatter pass by her closed door. She had been in a bad mood ever since the warning, then when Sean up, that she had drowned herself in the work to stay ahead. She was a fast reader, sure, but even some of things she had to edit were a joke. But she had a feeling that Mr. Kelly did this as his way of *'be late again and I won't be so nice'* punishment, it did give her a good laugh though so she wasn't too bored. There was a knock on the door, which puzzled her, but when the door opened it was Conner. Another person she truly didn't feel like seeing right now.

"I'm busy, Conner." She told him, as she out the pencil in her ear and bit on the straw she had been gnawing on for the past hour. He seemed shy, embarrassed, intimidated even, which made her laugh, which startled him. "For such a bright man, you sure falter in front of me." She said allowed to him, causing him to chuckle nervously.

"Boss sent me here. Said you haven't answered..."

"Don't have my phone. Have to work late cause of him. What other excuse…"

"He's worried…"

"Don't care. I have work to do so…"

"He'll be down…"

"No and that is final. Tell him to go home and play happy bachelor at home. He obviously wants to do that instead. Just go." She said to him, her face set and stone. She was done playing all these games. Tired of being treated like a child. The man nodded his head, closing the door behind him, as she let out a small frustrated scream. She was done with it all. His supposed promises of being there, when he always seemed to leave her. She hit the desk with her fist, cursing under her breathe as the pain that shot through her, as she set back to work.

It had been a bit after nine, by the clock on her computer, when she finally packed her things up for the day. She noticed, as she headed to the elevators, that her boss was on the phone with someone. He waved at her, before turning around in his chair. Shrugging her shoulders, she pressed the down button and got on once the doors opened. It didn't take long for the cart to arrive at garage level, as she walked over to get Harley. Hopping onto it, as she put her hair into a tight ponytail; the helmet she had forgotten at home in her rush to be here this morning, as she started her bike up. It purred to life, as she sped off into the busy streets. She didn't bother going straight home, but instead went to a bar. After all she was only going for a few drinks, but instead got a few cocktails that she could taste the rum in it. She paid the tab, watching whatever game was on currently, after downing some shots. A part of her wished she had her phone, but thankfully she didn't. She left the bar, hopped back onto her Harley and sped off into the night air. Her old rebellious ways were coming back. It made her feel happier and much more at ease, as she finally made her way back home a few hours later. Never once noticing the familiar car that Conner drove the whole entire time.

Opening up the door to her apartment, after fumbling with her keys, she staggered inside after slamming it closed. Turning on the lights, she stopped dead in her tracks at the familiar site of her ex-boyfriend. The drunken stupor she had been no longer there, her phone miraculously on the table besides her. But the only thing, as she texted help to Sean and Conner, was how he got here; among other questions. She saw him walk over to him, the smell of cheap beer and stale cigarettes invading her nostrils. A devilish smile on his face, as he stood in front of her. The crumpled note, that Sean had written for her, in his hands.

"Bitch thought she could dance with the devil eh?" His voice raspier and harsher than last she heard of. Her heart was pounding in her chest, as his finger traced her jawline. A silent prayer of hope being raised up, for both men to come here and quick. She just hoped they bring the police, but that would be too much. Either way, she had to stall him, somehow. Someway she had think of something, anything. Moving away from him seemed futile, especially when he had cat like reflexes. His hands were now at her sides, trying to raise her shirt up but she lifted up a knee to knee him again, but he anticipated it. A dark heady laughter spewed out of his mouth. Fear was beginning to eat her up as the seconds ticked by, the minutes felt like hours, as it felt like a dance of cat and mouse. A dance of when he'd take his first strike.

"Why are you..."

"To finish what I..."

"No! I don't want you, you sick twisted bastard!" She said through gritted teeth, but it seemed to only make him laugh as if she as telling him a joke. It only made her feel worse. All she wanted to do was come home and drink, but this wasn't what she had expected. The question came back again, as she backed up towards the wall, as to why he was here. How he got out of jail, and why he wouldn't leave her alone. The smirk on his face turned psychotic as if he finally caught his pray. He kissed her earlobe, making her shiver with disgust, but as he pressed his body up against her, it had the exact opposite effect on him. She tried to wiggle, tried everything in her power to get out of his grasp, but he grabbed her wrists so hard she knew it'd have bruises on them before too long. Her thoughts becoming more scrambled as her hope to be rescued slowly diminished by the second. His tongue felt like sand paper to her skin, nothing like Sean's. The tears slowly came falling from her eyes as she yelled out for help.

She opened her eyes, as he tried to gag her, something she never liked in the process, as he ripped her pants off of her, the button falling to the ground, the zipper flying to God knows where. She bit his finger, but it did no use. The grasp on her became even harsher, as she screamed for help once again. The walls were paper thin, she had figured that out awhile back. But still no help came, her tears were streaming down her face, as he started pile driving inside of her. It was brutal, harsh even. Her sobs racked her body, just as the door was caved in and a gush of wind was felt. She didn't know what was going on, but she heard shouts, as she wrapped herself in a fetal position. Her world seemed to crash in around her, as the dark consumed her. Leaving all thought and reason behind, as the drunk stupor finally got to her and the events that had followed after.

CHAPTER 18

THE DAY HAD STARTED early for him, they always did, and he didn't want to disturb Emily as she slept peacefully next to him. His phone alarm was vibrating next to him, it was a little after four in the morning, he had to be at the office early today, because of a meeting with some of the boards. He didn't get why it had to be at six, but he needed to get ready for the day regardless. Turning off the alarm, not only for his phone, but Emily's alarm clock as well he got up, after carefully moving her arm from his waist. She mumbled incoherently in her sleep, before laying on her other side. The birds and the flower showing in the dim light of the room. He got up, went into the other room, looking for some paper. It took him ages to find some, when really it didn't take long at all, as he wrote a brief message on it. He put the pen down, reading over what he had wrote down, as he placed his jacket over his shoulder. The city lights shining brightly through the opened curtain in the living room, which stopped him in his tracks for a moment. He wondered if they had been pulled back last night, or if they had been closed. A slight frown formed on his face, but he wasn't going to read too much into it right now.

Walking back into her bedroom, he set the note down on her side table. He watched her sleep for a few minutes more, before leaning down and kissing her forehead. It was amazing how peaceful she looked in her sleep, no worry etched her face at all like it did when she was awake. Putting on his shoes, he knew this would be a long day, hoping she wouldn't get to mad at him for letting her sleep without waking her up. He saw the sleeping pills, which seemed to have only been used once or twice. Shaking his head, he wished that she would take them, though he wasn't going to beg her to do so especially when she was a ticking time bomb at times. Chuckling lightly at the irony of his words, as he tucked the covers in around her.

"Sleep tight my angel." He whispered in her ear, kissing under the lobe, before making sure everything had been in place. The note lay there, seemingly untouched as if he had never placed it there a few minutes ago. He picked it up, re-reading it over to make sure she understood his reasoning of leaving her so early, before folding it up and placing it under the antique looking lamp. The note read...

Em,

Sorry I didn't wake you, but you looked so peaceful and it's early right now. Please don't get to mad when you realize you've woken up so late. Take the day off to rest. I must go in early for a meeting. Something you love to call boring and dull.

Yours,
Sean

As he walked back into the living room he thought he saw a shadow of a figure, but when he looked he didn't see anything when he looked closely. He scratched his head, as he texted several of his men to watch Emily's place closely just in case he hadn't been imagining things. He had a bad feeling and a part of him wanted to stay, but knew this meeting was important for his business. Sighing, as he got a reply back from David saying that at least five of his security was watching the apartment building, but in discrete places. He breathed a sigh of relief before leaving the apartment, and instead of taking the elevator he went down the stairwell instead.

He was thankful, when he saw his men surrounding David when he got to the garage level. He nodded at them, as he was handed a clean suit from Conner. He clapped him on the back, seeing the obvious worry in his eyes. There was definitely something going on, and he wasn't sure if he wanted to hear the news, but this was his girl they were talking about, and it did concern him. Very much so!

"Boss, her ex escaped from jail a day and a half ago. The cops have put a warrant out for his arrest. I know you have a busy day today but maybe…" one of the newer guys said, but stopped mid-sentence from the look he was giving him.

"John, if that bastard lays a finger on my girl I'll cut off his nuts myself. And you all know that I can't cancel with the boards. You just better keep a fucking close eye on her and her place today. No excuses!" He said them all, his voice in a stern but in a warning tone. He made eye contact with them all, particularly with Emily's bodyguard as he nodded profusely. He didn't want to show his obvious worry, but it was hard not to show in front of these guys. They were always there for him, but this was the first time they were told to protect his girl. He ran a hand through his hair, before the guys all told him to let him handle it. He nodded, as he walked to his Lamborghini and started up the engine. This was going to be one long day. He thought to himself, as he drove off towards his building where he was going to wash up and change there. He was thankful for the bathroom his office had. It had been a useful companion over the years.

Once he got to the building, he immediately went to the elevator and pressed the top floor button. He knew his PA's wouldn't be here till closer to the meeting would take place. The doors pinged open, to his level, and walked to his office. The security lights were on, which he turned off and turned on the actual ones. He walked to the left of the room, headed into the bathroom and took a brief shower before getting ready for the day. As he sat down at his desk, looking at some of the paperwork that needed his attention, his thoughts going back to Emily. He hoped she was okay, but he knew his guys would call him if something had been amiss. He trusted them to do so, and if they didn't he'd fire them on the spot. No questions asked either.

The hours went by, the meeting with the boards seemed to drag on forever, but they had long since agreed on the things that needed to be changed with the company, but most of them started talking

R. A. B.

about golf and other things. He wasn't in the mood to hear about
personal talk, but he wasn't going to rush them out of the conference
room either. David had texted him, a few times, saying that no one
had entered the building that looked like him. Nor did anyone force
entry into her bedroom window. It puzzled him, but he knew better
to let his guard down. They all did for that matter. The elder man,
then stood up, finally dismissing the meeting that had long been
over. Shaking hands with all of the men, he noticed it a bit past noon
when he finally entered into his office again.

"Sir!" Conner came into his office, not even five minutes after he had
sat down in his chair. He bolted straight out of his chair, wondering
why he wasn't on watch.

"Why aren't you…"

"She is here, working. Livid I might add!" Conner said to him, as if
this wasn't an obvious reason why he was here. He scratched his
face, feeling the obvious stubble that was there, before sighing.
At *least* she wasn't at home where that man could be waiting to
strike at any given time. He just hoped that she had seen the note
he left her but it was obvious that hadn't been the case, if her own
bodyguard said that she was livid.

"What do you mean, livid?" He asked after a brief pause as he paced
back and forth. He wondered why she didn't come up here, but knew
that her own boss on the editing floor would give her a warning. If
not, he would have some words with Mr. Kelly himself. He knew one
thing he'd have to talk to her before it was too late, but even so he
didn't want to worry her either. He let out a sigh, before stopping
mid pace and looked at Conner; waiting for him his response.

"As in, she took the Harley without her helmet, and dressed in casual
clothes, sir." He said to him, almost apologetically. He gritted his
teeth, knowing from that he would leave her be for now. It was
always best to let her calm down for a bit before approaching her,
even that didn't always work. He nodded his head, walking back
towards his desk, and leaned against it. He wasn't going to show
his obvious worry for his girl in front of her bodyguard, but they all

knew better than to not realize he cared for her deeply. He didn't want to admit it, but it was true. He just needed to get past the pride that Emily always had, and get to the root of the problem; why she couldn't fully open up to him. He rubbed his chin, knowing if he didn't stop the worrying he wouldn't get any work done, not that he didn't do much to begin with since the meeting took up half of his morning. He thought somewhat amused by the irony of it all.

"Thanks, you may go. But if anything is..."

"Amiss, we will all let you know. David already told us, boss." Conner said, with a nod as he walked out of his office. He walked around his desk, opening up the balcony door, and walked onto the small platform that overlooked the city. He could see everything today, since it was a clear day and not a cloud in the sky. The sun felt warm, with a promise of better days to come, but right now seemed cloudy in his eyes; especially with the whole Isabelle situation and now with this mark character. He sighed, wondering why the exes wanted to come out of the wood works now and if she had any connection with his escape from the jailhouse. A sinking feeling came to him as he wondered, but if that were the case she would've gloated about it? Maybe? He shook his head at the thought, not even wanting to think about it. Hell, she didn't even know about Emily till a few days ago. That was a particular memory he really didn't feel like remembering ever again.

She had come to him in the middle of the work day. His desk was littered with papers of things that needed his attention, and what could possibly be thrown away. He rubbed his temple, wishing it was time to go home. To her, they had planned a special evening of just them; dinner and a movie. A classic romantic evening, without any interruptions. At least he hoped was the case. But he looked up as there was a bunch of noise going on outside of his office door. What could possibly be going on? He wondered, as he put the pen down onto his desk as the door opened, revealing Isabelle in a tight fitted skirt with a shirt so tight her boobs could fall out of it at any given second. He looked at both Lucy and Pam who both seemed at a loss for words behind her. He sighed, leaned back in his chair, before nodding his head. The only other person, besides them, in the room was David. She didn't even bat an eyelid at his head of security. It was if she pretended they were the only two in the room.

"What do you want, Belle?" he said after she didn't say anything at all. He really didn't feel like seeing her, or smell her over expensive perfume that seemed to fill the air quicker than anything he smelled before. It was a rather nauseating smell in fact, that he felt like he had to hold his breathe.

"I want you to drop this silliness and be mine again." She said after a small pause, causing not only him but David to bark in laughter. She was out of her mind, if she ever though to ever happen again. He thought to himself, as he finally controlled himself long enough to not laugh anymore.

"Not happening. Ever. I'm with someone who I am...'

"What do you see in her anyways?" She asked in a purr like voice, which only just made his insides crawl with disgust. Was she that blind not to see how different she was from her? Or was this just an act to use against him. Either way he didn't like how this whole conversation was going, or he could tell that David was about ready to escort her out but he shook his head briefly. He wanted to see what happened. He wasn't sure why but he wanted to see what her game was.

"I see a brighter future than..."

"She's not a looker like me..."

"More like a hooker if you ask me." Came David's response, from where he was sitting at, in the background. He chuckled at the statement, as Isabelle came over to him, sitting down right in front of his chair, leaning over. It seemed as if she didn't even hear what had just been said. He stared her right in the eyes; hazel to green.

"You'll want me back before too long, Seanie." She said, leaning over to kiss him, but moved his chair over to the left before she could do just that. She giggled, girlishly as she always had done, before getting up off of the desk and instead of leaving, she sat down on his lap trying to press her suit on him, but in a matter of seconds David had put her in handcuffs and escorted her out of his office. To say he didn't hear her profanities all the way down the hall, into the elevator was an understatement.

The last of her words played over in his head like no other, as he texted David about it, wondering if he thought about the same thing or not. He would deal with Emily soon, but first he had to do some research before he went down to the twenty first floor to see her. He sat down in his chair, wondering what had happened to make Isabelle search so deep into Emily's past to bring back an ex-boyfriend, whom by the looks of things had kept a very dark and dangerous past away from said woman. Looks were definitely deceiving and this man had fooled her. Maybe that was part of the reason Emily had been so reserved, so held back on letting him in. He hated the thought, hated the feeling it gave him just thinking about it. He put the password into his laptop and set to work on what he could find, if anything on if the two were connected somehow and someway.

The day wore on, so did the minutes and hours it seemed like as well. The conversation hadn't gone as planned with Emily, and he wasn't even sure if they were still together or not. There was a bruise forming on his cheek, from where she had punched him earlier had formed, but he wasn't going to say how or why it happened. It wasn't anyone's business, even though David had a good laugh over it, which he still didn't think was too funny in the first place. None of them had come back to him on anything and he hadn't gotten any closer to finding out if the two were connected someway or not. He sighed heavily, as the sun started to set for the day, leaving a heavy glare on his computer screen, as he wrote some things down on paper. Both Lucy and Pam had left early for the day for some kind of double date thing, he couldn't really remember but he just hoped they had a good time. He remembered the last time they had tried that and ended up being in sour moods all day long, and he didn't feel like dealing with another repeat of that.

"She hasn't left yet." Came the voice of John, one of the men who had been watching the garage of this building since she had come earlier today. He had informed everyone, including him that she would be late. According to her it was his fault, but if she had just read the note she would've still been at her apartment having the time to herself, and yet he was glad she didn't at the same time. It was almost like a no win scenario, only this time it was a win win situation for everyone, or at least until that dirty little rat was caught, because so far it was as if this Mark guy *knew* how to avoid them all. Which didn't help the fact he was worried sick about what would happen if he was there waiting in this building or wherever else. He rubbed his stubble on his chin, before he heard one of the men telling John what he had said earlier on that day. *Idiot I swear.* He thought to himself, as he started sorting out things that needed his attention now or later, before turning his laptop off for the day. The whole thing seemed a bit fishy to him, and he hated not knowing what was going on.

Getting up from his chair, he looked out the window, the shadows of the sun dancing on some of the building as the sky slowly turned into night. He saw the many cars, in a traffic jam below, people walking around looking like ants from so far up and any one of them could be him. It was maddening, as he heard the special text tone come from his phone, meaning Emily was trying to reach him. He walked over to his desk, almost dropping it in the process. The words; **HELP!!!** dancing in his face. He put his jacket on, as he ran out of his office as quick as his legs could take him. He took to the stairs instead, not bothering waiting for an elevator.

"Conner! David! He's there!" He said jumping down stairwells, as he yelled out into the phone. His voice echoing in the stairwell of the stairs, as he finally opened a door to what looked like the eighteenth floor, he wasn't really sure since he didn't look at the number that closely, as he pressed the down button to get on the next available elevator as he caught his breathe as well. He placed his head against the metal of the cart, willing it to go faster. He didn't even want to imagine what was going on! He thought as he gritted his teeth, slamming the wall next to him. The ping sounded, and even before the doors were all the way open he ran immediately to his car, starting it up and drove out of the underground garage to her apartment building.

He got there, just as he saw a couple of his guys talking to the police, they had done their part, but he didn't want to chat with any one of them right now. Once his door was closed, he saw David come up behind him, with a few policemen behind them and they made their way up to her floor of the building. Luckily, it didn't take along but to him it seemed like an eternity. The moment the doors pinged open, he ran down the hallway as the screams for help could be heard. The police had their guns drawn, his heart racing as they started to push the door open with their bodies. It was like a slow moving movie, where everything seemed to go in slow motion with the events that were happening. The door was caved in, and he pushed his way through as he saw the monster of a man raping her against the wall. Her voice was a cry of help, as he pushed him away from her.

"You have no right to call the police on me." Mark said as he sneered at him. A sickening grin plastered on his face. The cops were circled around them, their guns drawn at the man before him, so he had nowhere to run as they glared at each other. He wanted to punch him so badly, but kept his composure for now.

"You just raped my girlfriend." He said, through clenched teeth. He was itching so bad just to strike him, cause him pain like he had done to her, but knew his status of being a CEO of a company would be troublesome in the courts, regardless if he was wealthy or poor. Mark laughed haughtily at him, as if he thought it were a joke. His eyes danced with mirth not of anything else.

"The bitch is useless now. Always was. Now she's really damaged goods." He laughed as if telling a joke. The cops finally moved into action, as they all heard enough, handcuffing him on the spot. He immediately went to Emily's side, as a stretcher was brought in to take her to the hospital. He wrapped the blanket tightly around her body, as he noticed the stench of alcohol coming from her labored breathing. He sighed inwardly knowing this was going to be the ultimate test for them, at least for now it was. He squeezed her hand knowing that worrying about it right now wouldn't do any good, as he felt David's familiar hand on his shoulder, as he brushed a stray hair off of her face. She looked so peaceful in her inebriated state, but he knew that was only just from the shock and drunken state she was in.

"David grab my stuff from my office, Conner pick out some comfortable clothes for Emily to wear, Troy tell the rest of the guys to see how the asshole got into this place. There must be an insider in on this. I smell a rat. I'll be at the hospital with Emily." He said after a beat, watching the three men nod their heads as he followed the paramedics down the hall and into the waiting elevator. He noticed the curious heads peeping out of their doors, whispers even, but they didn't ask what was going on. He heard the beeping of the machine, they had hooked up to her, as the doors finally shut around them. Her heartbeat sounded fine, so did everything else. At least from he could tell, though he wasn't an expert in the field of medicine. The doors reopened a few minutes later, and they immediately rushed to the waiting ambulance and to whatever hospital that was the closest by them.

CHAPTER 19

BEEPING WAS THE ONLY sound she could hear at first, a few hushed whispers as well as she opened her eyes to a blinding white ceiling light. Her muscles ached, her head pounded, and all she wanted to do was throw up. She looked to her left, seeing the blinds were drawn, the first of the day's rays trying to soak through them, before realizing the beeping had to do with the machine next to her. Why was she in a hospital for? She wondered to herself, as she looked to her right to see Sean and her dad there. The events of last night were hazy but the soreness was there every time she had moved. Had she been in a wreck? Was her motorcycle okay? The millions of thoughts were racing through her head like a sore thumb. It didn't help the fact she already had a headache from the alcohol she had consumed lady night.

The hushed whispers stopped, as they both came to her side. The fact her dad was here was also astounding to her, especially when he was a cop who never missed a day of work, unless something major happened. It wasn't often that he did, but he had tons of vacation time and was always welcomed in her eyes. Her mom however, was the exact opposite. She always seemed to think of only herself, and would only come when it was convenient for herself. She had tried keeping them together, as a kid, but it was a futile thing to do. Her dad wiped some of her hair out of her, as she moved in a comfortable position; even though every time she tried her body ached. The door opened, revealing a nurse with a chart in hand, as she checked everything on the monitor, before leaving again. Oh how she hated hospitals! She thought to herself.

"Daddy, what're you doing here?" She finally said, noticing how rough she sounded. Did the alcohol affect her that badly? She wondered curiously feeling puzzled, as she looked at Sean, raising her hand to him and he took it squeezing it tightly. He had always been good to her, always.

"Do you remember anything from last night?" He asked her, his voice sharper in person than it was on the phone. He had been in the military, didn't take shit from no one, and could either be your best friend or your worst enemy in seconds. He had a buzz cut, that didn't even look like a haircut anymore. He was handsome, but you could tell he had seen some things in his days. He had never remarried, and she thought of him as her role model regardless of all the times they bitched and bickered at one another.

"Other than leaving work and going for a drink, not really." She said to him, as if this was a no brainer. There was a knock on the door, revealing another nurse, maybe doctor, she never could tell the difference really. It was a man this time, he had jet black hair, piercing green eyes, and a pearly white smile. He seemed a bit intimidated by the two powerful men in the room, causing her to giggle at the thought. Sean looked at her confused, but didn't say anything more.

"Miss Night, my name is Randy Hotch, and I'm your attending doctor today. How do you feel?" He asked stiffly, as if he was bored at the simple question. She rolled her eyes, they all seemed the same. Bored and lame.

"Well, *Randy,* if you must ask I'm peachy king. The..."

"Emily Renee Night." Her father's voice of warning came. He hated her smartass mouth, always had and forever will. She sighed, before crossing her arms, pouting.

"I'm sore, if you care to know. I'm not sure why, unless I wrecked my bike again." She said as if this was a no brainer, even though the last time she had done so she was in casts all over her body. Or most of it anyways.

"Do you know Mark Sayer?" He finally asked, as if he wanted to cut to the chase. The mention of her exes name gave her a sinking sick feeling in the pit of her stomach. Blurry images seemed to come to her mind, causing her to panic as tears came to her eyes. Her father immediately held her in his arms, as the images came flooding back to her.

"He's my ex. Don't tell me..."

"The soreness would be from him raping you, miss. We did..."

"I know you did the whole test thing. Not the..." She trailed off, shaking her head as old images came flooding back to her. Back to the time she was in high school, at an old friend's party, and she didn't want to think about it. Closing her eyes, she felt her father hold her closer. She daren't dare look Sean's way, after all she was damaged goods. Nothing but trouble for anyone really. At least that's how she felt anyways. She heard the door open, then close, but she didn't know if the man had left or not. She wanted the images of old, and the hazy ones from yesterday to go away. But even so that was a wishful thought.

"Em..." She heard Sean's voice, small and unsure. She shook her head, knowing the tears were soaking through her dad's shirt.

"It's okay he won't hurt..."

"How the hell do you know that dad? Every man I've been..."

"I trust him, sweetheart. He called me the moment you were admitted in. He really does care about you." Her dad told him, but she didn't want to believe him. Too much shit had happened in her life to believe such things. But even so, she had felt even more alive whenever she was around him, than any of her past relationships she's ever been in. She looked over at Sean, who look crestfallen at the scene before him. He looked powerless, but at the same time powerful. Sighing inwardly, she squeezed his hand but that was

R. A. B.

it. She just couldn't shake the feeling he'd hurt her in some way or another, but deep down she knew he never would. He was one of the highest grossing billionaires on the east coast in the past several years, she had done the research. His power, and wealth intimidated her.

She stayed in her dads arms, for a good while, before laying back down on the bed. The police had come and gone, telling her he had picked the lock on her door and that he was now in maximum security in Texas. They had flown him back, last night, on a plane with at least ten cops. She was glad, weary of the whole situation, but was happy nevertheless. The same doctor had come back to tell her that she'd be able to leave tomorrow. It didn't matter really, as she closed her eyes to rest. The soft tapping coming from Sean's laptop could be heard, the beeping from the machine no longer on, which she was thankful. It had been annoying to listen to anyways. The TV was on low, but neither one of them were talking to the other. Her father had left to go site seeing, not too long ago, but even so she knew it was to give them some alone time.

"Sean. Don't look so serious." She said to him, as she slowly made her way over to where he sat in the chair. He scooted his chair back, as she climbed onto his lap, breathing in his scent she had grown to like so much, as he wrapped his arms around her. She laid her head on his chest, hearing his heart beat.

"I'm just worried about..."

"I'll be alright. I'm a big girl." She told him looking up at him, giving him a brief kiss on the lips as she looked at his computer screen. A bunch of numbers were on an excel sheet, with a few other things. She didn't bother asking why he was doing the accounting job, after all he was the CEO and could do whatever he pleased with his company. She just hoped that this didn't put him behind schedule, even though it was the weekend. To her, he seemed very dedicated to his work and from the looks of things would continue to do so.

"I promised your dad I'd take care of..."

"Don't make promises that you can't..."

"Emily do you honestly believe I'm going to hurt you? Have I given you any reason to think or believe I will?" He said to her, closing the lid to his laptop and turning her around so they were face to face. She picked at a string on his shirt, before sighing, almost defeated like. She had never felt as vulnerable as she did now, it wasn't a particular emotion she was used to and hated the feeling of it now. She got up, walking over to the window that had a view of the city, as a few tears escaped from her eyes. She didn't want him seeing her like this, or ever for that matter. She wiped away the tears, pretending her nose was itching, as she looked at ocean from afar.

"What did my dad say to you, Sean?" She asked after a few minutes of complete silence. The sun sparkling on the water in the distance, the tiny black specs she assumed were that of ships in the distance coming into the harbor soon. She didn't feel like talking about them. Not right now at least. She just didn't want to feel like that he had some obligation to be with her, especially if she knew how her father operated. He may have the best interests at heart, but sometimes she wondered. It was easy growing up with her father, especially with his military background. Hell, he had been a sergeant and a corporal at one point in time.

"He said to take care of my little girl and I plan..."

"Don't make promises you can't keep. You don't..."

"You don't get it do you?" He asked her, as he walked over to her standing next to her. He turned her around, so that they were facing each other. She looked at him, but gave nothing away. She knew how to pull a blank face when need be.

"Get what? That you want to get on my dad's good graces or..."

"Emily I've wanted you since the first day we met. You need..."

"No you need to realize not everyone needs to be saved. I'm beyond it, I've been broken and..."

"You honestly think that?" He asked, as he stepped closer to her, as she stepped back a step. He sighed, as if he was frustrated with how this was going. She didn't think she needed to be saved. How could she be, when she was so used to being hurt and rejected? Did he really think that she could believe he was different than the rest? Especially when she had heard the same bullshit in the past? She wondered to herself, as he made another attempt to get near her. She didn't move this time, but made no attempt to touch him either. He wrapped his arms around her, kissing the top of her forehead.

"I'm not sure what to think. Is that what you want to hear?" She asked him, after several minutes of silence, before kissing him briefly on the lips once more. She yawned a little, as he guided her back to the bed, not saying anything but it didn't seem uncomfortable or awkward at all.

"I want you to trust me. But it seems..."

"Seems like what?! Look we didn't have to get into this relationship Sean. You are a hot shot billionaire that owns a damn empire for Christ's sake! You could have any girl..."

"I only want you and...."

"Hah! Sounds like bullshit to me, *sir.*" She said to him before laughing at the audacity this man had, as she shook her head at the whole thing. He seems so *sure* of himself, that it was as if a broken record was starting to spin. Yet, none of her past boyfriends ever got acquainted with her father either. They had all been intimidated by him, his glare alone seem to put a horn dogs tail in between their legs in a matter of seconds. She could tell he was getting annoyed by the whole thing, as his phone started ringing. He looked down at it, before putting it back in his pocket.

"Emily you've got to be the most stubborn woman I've ever met!" He said as the door opened, revealing her father. His ever present stern glare set on his face. She could see he was assessing the situation before him, before walking over to Sean and clapping him on the shoulder. It was a rather odd sight to see, especially when he was never won over that quickly, by anyone ever. She sighed, as she smiled sweetly at him.

"I may be your father, young one, **but** I will kick your butt if you don't give this man a chance! And don't you dare interrupt me either! This man may be a billionaire hot shot CEO, or whatever the hell you think he is, but he's one classy guy. And yes, you're one stubborn woman. Get it from your mother." Her father said to her, making her feel like an adolescent child, which she wasn't too keen on feeling like that. At all. She sighed, knowing he was right. He always was.

"Yes, sir." She said in a small voice, as he leaned over the bed to give her a hug. She had a feeling he wasn't going to stay long, his job didn't wait. Hell, the bad guys didn't take the day off on account of him being gone.

"I'll see you later baby." He kissed her forehead, before walking over to where Sean was and they shook hands, a silent understanding passing between them. She could only imagine what it had been about. "You take care of her kid. And thanks for letting me use your private jet to get back home." He finished, causing her to fume inside. How dare he flaunt his wealth in her dads face like that! She thought to herself, as she glared at the two of them. She didn't know what to think, but she sure as hell wasn't going to just jump at the man's feet because of it. Shaking her head, she decided to play along with their game. If the CEO wanted to use money, to convince her father that he was the *one* for her, then she would go along with it. For now.

"*Fine*, if you want things to *work* between us, then I'll give him..."

"If you think he paid me his money, young lady, then you're greatly mistaken. Are you with him for his..."

"With him for his money? Oh my gosh I could give a shit less about it. I could live in a bungalow and wouldn't..."

"Speaking of living. I moved you into a penthouse..."

"Dad! You can't just move me into a..." She paused, not bothering saying anymore. Oh how she wished she could get out of this hospital room now. It was driving her crazy, looking at the four walls, and seeing her father take control of things was something she had never been fond of. Hell, for all she knew he could've paid an entire years rent to the people of the building. It wasn't the first time he had done something like that. He had the money to do it, but he had always pretended it wasn't there in his bank account. Something she sometimes had a problem with; thus all the new cars and clothes as of late. Her father had gone to the casinos and was always amazing at the machines, he never expected to win, but he always managed to do so. She had asked, at one point in time, what his trick was, but he had just smiled at her and pointed to his forehead. To this day, he had never given her his trick, which she was sure was just because he knew how to work the machines and she didn't.

"It's better than what you had. I best be off." He said to them, as he walked over to the closed door, opened it up before turning to face the both of them again. "Give him a chance, Emily." He said giving her a smile. She hopped off of the bed, giving him a hug, hating the fact he was leaving so soon, but she knew his job needed him as well. His visits were always short, but always full of wisdom. He rubbed her back, as he shook Sean's hand once more.

"Take care of yourself, Paul." He said to him, before her father left the room. It was just them again and she was dying to get out of here. Sure, it had been almost a day since the event happened, but she didn't want to stay in the confines of this room any longer. Walking over to the table, where her new keys to her place were at, an envelope sat next to it. She opened it up, seeing his cursive scrawl with *at least* a thousand dollars inside of it. Shaking her head, she knew he meant well but she hated when he did that to her. Giving her money, even though he knew she had plenty in her account. He had made sure of it, even though she didn't have the heart to tell him that she dumped most of it back into his savings account. He never *really* checked it anyways, so she didn't have to answer to his questions about it. She unfolded the note, and began to read it;

Emily,

I know you've always despised hearing the truth from your old man,
but I will be brief with my words. You need to stop letting the past
get to you, and see that the man has your best interests at heart.
At first, when I heard who you were dating I thought you were with
him for his money. But my Emmy pie isn't one for that. Don't be so
stubborn and let your heart guide you for once. That brain of yours is
a trip. Take your insomnia pills too. Send the cash on something nice.

Love,
Dad

She re-read the note over, laughing a little before throwing it into the trashcan. She looked over at the man who seemed so out of place, so out of character for such a popular man of the business world. She really did care about him, but her father's words were easier said than done. That heart of hers had been broken numerous times in the past, beyond repair it seemed like, but even so she knew if she didn't give him the chance he deserved, he'd leave. It amazed her that he hadn't already with her being as stubborn as she is. There was a knock on the door, taking her out of her reverie, as the doctor came into the room. She frowned not sure why he was back in here, but she had a feeling her father had done something to get her out of here.

"You'll be discharged within the hour. Your father is…"

"A very convincing man who won't be told no?" She asked, laughing at the look the male nurse had on his face. He still seemed like he was bored and did t want to be here. She had a feeling, not only did her father work his magic but Sean had done the same again, seeing as he didn't even bother looking his way. The man didn't seem amused at all.

"Yes." He said stiffly, causing her to bite her tongue to not say something sassy. Not that she ever really cared in the first place, but he was truly a bore and needed to do something to get that stiff look off of his face.

"Okay stiff you can skedaddle now. Maybe what you need to get that boring look off your face, is a good fuck. I mean..."

"Emily!" Came Sean's shocked voice, which only made her flip him off and smile at him. He shook his head, before going back to whatever he was doing on his laptop. She had a feeling it was probably to do with her safety. She gritted her teeth just thinking about it. She be damned if she couldn't drive herself to and from places. What she wanted was to drive her Yamaha for a good spin, it had been awhile after all.

"Just speaking the truth, *babe.*" She said to him with a wink. The man muttered something under his breathe, before leaving the room. She noticed Sean was glued to his computer screen, tapping away furiously. Whatever it was, it didn't seem pretty, so she didn't feel like bothering him at all. Picking up the remote, for the TV, she flipped through the channels till she found something worth watching; The Wolverine. She loved Hugh Jackman, and always wanted to meet him. After all he was one of her favorite actors, George Clooney happened to her all-time favorite, both were major hunks in her eyes.

That afternoon, as she headed towards her newest apartment; the penthouse suite, she wondered why Sean had been so quiet. Sure, he would touch her waist, playfully grab her ass, and kiss her but something was off about him. Like there was something on his mind, but she wasn't sure if she should ask or leave it be. Surely, if it had to do with her, he would tell her right? She thought to herself, as the elevator doors opened up to her new place. There was an open foyer, leading to a wide opened space that looked like the living room, off to the right the kitchen could be seen. A set of stairs, to the left, that she assumed led to her bedroom and a few others. Walking further in, she noticed a bookcase filled with books, on the far left that was surrounded by a door. She let go of his hand, as she walked over to it, gracing some of the spines with her fingers, before opening the closed door. She gasped, as she saw even more books, on a bookshelf. A chair, couch, and a mini bar happened to be in there. Chuckling at the thought, she noticed that all of her favorite drinks happened to be there. She knew, from experience, getting drunk and reading at the same time wasn't a good thing. She saw a mini fridge, but nothing was in it, which she was thankful for.

Walking out of the room, completely ignoring the fact that Sean was on the phone with someone, she headed up the stairs, after checking out the fireplace that happened to have ready logs in it. Winter would be here soon, a few months in fact, and she had a feeling she'd be in front of it a lot. She noticed, once she had reached the landing of the second floor, there was three separate doors. The first one seemed to be her office, by the way it was laid out, the computer seemed to be high tech, and she noticed this room also had several book shelves of books. It was as if she was in a dream, a dream that her father had somehow miraculously happened over such a short time, though she had a feeling he had help with it. Closing the door, she opened the next one; a game room. She laughed, seeing the fuse-ball table, air hockey table, pool table, and a basketball hoop inside of it. It was as if living back at home, but not so in a way. She looked towards the door, noticing that Sean was standing there, his hands in his pockets. He looked like a little kid, waiting at the door for her. Smiling, she walked over to him, giving him a brief kiss on the lips.

"Thank you." She whispered against his lips, before walking around him and towards the last room. She knew, before opening it up it'd be her new bedroom. She wasn't sure what to expect, but she had a feeling she'd be shocked by it.

"Are you going..."

"No I felt like just staring at this door all day long, just for shits and giggles." She said to him sarcastically, as she looked up at him. He glared at her playfully before shaking his head. Just because he saw her *almost* soft side at the hospital, didn't mean he was going to get that all the time.

Turning the door knob, pushing it open, she felt like her jaw had dropped as she stepped into the room. It had a medieval, yet modern, look to it, the bed had a canopy around it, the drapes folded back against the posts. She ran her fingers over the wood, feeling the crevices under the tips of her fingers. There was a fireplace near the window, with a gate surrounding it that could be folded back for easy access to the logs inside. Walking towards the closet, pressing the button on the wall. revealing a walk in closet with a lot more clothes, shoes, heels than she had before. Looking over at Sean, he just shrugged as if he had no idea how they got there. Flipping him off, she pressed the button to the bathroom. It had a huge walk in shower to the far right, a Jacuzzi on her left, the toilet was in the middle. It too had the look the bedroom had as well, just more modernized. There was two sinks, with a large rectangular mirror above it, a cabinet for toiletries just to the right of it. Turning around she hugged him hard, kissing him passionately on the lips.

"You and my dad are sneaky bastards." She said after they had made it back down the stairs. He laughed as he gave her a cheeky smile, before leading her over to another closed door. She raised her eyebrow at him, wondering what he was hiding.

"I was going to wait…"

"Wait for what? Till I'm old and grey? Or…"

"You just had a…"

"Oh for the love of god don't treat me like a porcelain doll." She said to him, with her hands on her hips. He sighed, before he shrugged his shoulders and opened up the door. It was their own little room to play in, just like the one he had back at his place. She smirked at him, grabbing him by the crotch before releasing him.

"Not tonight maybe…"

"I was just messing with you. I know not tonight. Let's go out to eat and see a Broadway show." She said to him, hoping he wouldn't mind her suggestion. She hadn't been to one since she had been a kid, but she figured it was time to go to again. After all, she didn't live on Broadway Avenue just to live here. She had a feeling he had never even considered going to one either, so it was a perfect time for them both.

"I'll pick you up at seven then." He said to her, kissing her briefly on the lips, before leading them out of the room. It snapped shut behind them, he kissed her once more, before squeezing her hand. She watched him leave the penthouse, as she let out a breath she didn't realize she had been holding. It was a bit overwhelming to take in, but she was thankful for both of the men in her life, even if she had been content on just the apartment itself. She ran up the stairs, two at a time, and headed straight for her closet. She searched through the many dresses, before finding a white Halston Heritage Halter Dress with Layered Skirt and a pair of black Stuart Weitzman Mae Patent Platform Pump heels. She looked at herself in the mirror, hanging up on the back of the door, giving herself a thumbs up. Her hair was placed into a ponytail, as she made a mental note to get a haircut as soon as she could. She wanted the town to see her dressed up, looking amazing, on the arm of the most eligible bachelor of New York City.

CHAPTER 20

THE DAY HAD BEEN a long day, but he was thankful she had been to leave the hospital before nightfall. Her father, even though he seemed unsure of him at first, had given him a chance to explain himself. He understood his hesitation, though not the full reasoning behind it. Sure, Emily had a rough night the day before but at least *nothing* major had happened. He just wished he knew what had caused her to be so hesitant in trusting him, he had never given her any reason not to, but even so they both had pasts. Pasts that probably would change things between them, or bring them closer together. Hell, he promised her father he'd be there for Emily, and nothing would change that. As he pulled up into his drive, he noticed that David and John were having some kind of argument. There had been enough things going on as it was to even imagine what could possibly be wrong now. He parked his car, on the side of the house, and walked straight into the house. The smell of food coming from the kitchen, his house maid was busy preparing something amazing just by the smell and looks of it. He sighed, running his hands through his hair, knowing it had been awhile since he had stayed at home to enjoy her home cooking. Maybe if they ate here and then see a show it would work that way.

Picking up his phone, to dial her number, he heard the loud voices of the two men coming into the house. He set the phone down, as he crossed his arms in front of him waiting for some kind of explanation. *Hadn't there been enough mayhem for one day? One being last night and then Isabelle's attorney trying to press charges on him.* He thought to himself, sighing. He hadn't done anything so there was nothing to go on there, and his own attorney; the best in the field, had taken control the moment he mentioned something about it. It was only a matter of time that she would be revealed for who she truly was; a money hungry bitch. That's all she ever wanted from him, and he'd be damned if that happened again. He cleared his throat, waiting for the two whispering men, to explain themselves to him. They both looked towards him, seemingly embarrassed by the intrusion, but hell this was his house after all.

"Mind telling me what the fuck is going on with you two?" He asked them, looking from one to the other. He undid the tie, briefly glancing down at his watch to see the time, before looking back up. It almost six, he had plenty of time to get ready, especially when it didn't take him long to do so anyways.

"John has leaked..."

"You're fired. I don't need to have security who leaks anything, to anyone, at any given time. I'll make sure..."

"Sir, if you hear me out. I can..."

"No, you've been fired on the spot. David will see to it that you will never be in private security again. Have a nice rest of your evening though." He said, walking off towards his bedroom, slamming the door shut behind him. He couldn't believe a member of his staff had the balls to give things out about his private life. It was something he valued the most, keeping it tightly shut around men who knew to keep the secrets guarded. Luckily, for all of them, he hadn't been told the nitty gritty stuff, especially when he hadn't trusted him from the start. The yelling intensified, something seemed to have crashed onto the floor, which didn't bode well with him at all. Gritting his teeth, he reopened the door to see all of his men holding back David. This wasn't good at all.

"...you knew what kind of..."

R. A. B.

"What the fuck is going on in my house?! If I have to call the police..."

"They've already been called, sir." Said one of the men closest to him. He nodded his head, as he walked over to John, his fists clenched to the side. Apart of him knew he had some reason behind Isabelle's reappearance, and the other having to do with Mark escaping. He didn't realize the truth behind it all, till only just now. He could read in between the lines, even if he hated doing so at times.

"Handcuff him. I want everything he has frozen and liquidated from his name. Get my attorney involved." He said as he looked the man straight in the eyes, using a calm voice that held an underlying threat to it. He always won, no matter the situation. If someone threatened him, his empire, or people he knew he would take them down. He had done it before. Garrett, a fair skinned man, well built, and strawberry blonde hair produced some cuffs from his side, and handcuffed John straight away. He nodded at him, before putting his arm around the man and sat him down on the stool.

"Sir, I can explain..."

"NO! I DON'T WANT TO HEAR ANY EXPLANATION! OR YOUR SORRIES!" He bellowed, getting straight in the man's face, before feeling several of his guys pull him back. He shrugged them off, feeling his blood pressure rise slightly. "I have to get ready for my date with Emily. If you need me, just holler. Otherwise, just make sure this scum is gone!" He said to the others, after he had turned around to look at the rest of his men. They all seemed a bit shaken up, especially since they had never heard him yell before. He clapped a few on the shoulder, before heading back to his bedroom, closing the door with a snap. He undressed himself before getting into the hot shower spray, which helped to relax his tired wound up muscles. He didn't stay in there long, as he shaved his five o clock mess of a shadow and towel dried his body off.

Opening the closet doors, he had nothing but suits to the back, and shoes lined up in an organizer box. He wanted to pick one, that he hadn't worn in a while, which was hard cause he forgotten that some of them looked exactly alike. Chuckling to himself, he took one off the clothes rack, gently removing the hanger, as he put on the Jones New York Black Tic Vested Modern Fit Suit. He fixed his cuff links, before doing a Windsor knot. He looked hot if he did say so himself, the color of the suit seemed to really bring out his eyes, which he didn't care too much for but hey it was alright with him. Walking out of the room, he noticed the cops were taking away John, his attorney was present talking to some of the men. He sighed inwardly, not really wanting to have a legal conversation at the moment. Why couldn't he just enjoy his night? He wondered to himself, as they shook hands.

"William nice to see you." He said, politely even though he really wanted to just leave right now. The man chuckled clapping him on the back.

"You too, but I'll see you later. You have fun with your gal tonight. I'll handle this cluster fuck of a mess here." He said to him, with an understanding nod towards him. He smiled, as they shook hands once more, before leaving out the front door. There was *way* too much shit going on right now for his liking. He saw the police car take off, just as he stepped out of the house. He noticed that the Silver 2013 Hyundai Santa Fe Sport sat idle behind his Lamborghini, he hadn't seen Conner or Jacob in a while. But he noticed they were both in there. He would've had David with him, but he had his hands tied right now. Waving at the two guys, he got into his car, started up the engine before taking off down the street. He pressed Emily's name to call her, it was fifteen till seven.

"Hey I'm on my way. I just had shit to deal with but…"

"Everything okay? I mean we can go some…"

"Emily I don't want to cancel on you. Just had a rat in my crew, and my lawyer is involved. I rather…"

"It wasn't Conner was it? I've *grown* to like him." She said over the phone, causing him to laugh. At first she had hated having a security guard around her, not it seemed she finally understood. Maybe it had to do with the event that took place, or maybe it had to do with him. Either or he wasn't sure, but he wasn't going to question her motives over it.

"No, but I'll see you in a bit." He said before hanging up on her, after said had said bye to him on the phone. He revved up his engine, gaining a little speed on the highway towards the city before him. The sun had long since set for the day, the twinkling of the stars shining brightly above him, as he headed down highway 87 towards the inner parts of the city. He lived in Yonkers and always knew how to avoid traffic, but when it came down to it there was always going to be traffic. Thankfully though, he hadn't hit any heavy traffic yet.

The further he got into town, the city lights began to get brighter as he drove towards Broadway Avenue. It didn't take him long, even though it was a little after seven when he got to the front of the building. Emily had texted him saying she was waiting out front for him, and when he pulled up he saw how drop dead gorgeous she was. Her dress hugged her curves, the heels looked dangerous to him, her hair was up in a ponytail, and from what he could see she was wearing makeup. It was unusual to see her in makeup, and to be honest it was probably the only time he had seen her wear it. He got out of his car, opened the passenger side door for her, as she leaned in giving him a kiss on the lips before getting into the car. He had a sneaky suspicion that she was dressed up like this to make a statement to everyone, that she was his and no one could take him away from her. He smirked, as he looked towards the Nissan seeing both guys shake their heads. It was obvious they had figured it out as well. Waving them off, he got into the car as he drove down the street.

"Chinatown. Let's go there." She said without any hesitation. He smiled as he headed towards that area, avoiding what he could of the traffic, though it was impossible to do so when they ended up in several *almost* traffic jams.

They found, after parking somewhere close to the heart of Chinatown, a place to eat. It was amazing food, though it was always when he ventured down this way. Sure, they could've walked here, but it would've taken them longer especially in the heels she was wearing. He was thankful she was having a great time, it had been awhile since he saw a true smile play on her face. The other times had been rare, but she seemed more relaxed as he watched her flip off their security for the evening. He laughed, knowing that was her way of telling them hello. He looked behind him, seeing several people taking pictures of the two of them together. Luckily Conner and Jacob had confiscated the ones nearest to them, he figured it had to with Emily flipping them off, and he didn't feel like explaining that one the next day.

They finished their dinner, before heading towards the ticket booth to see what shows were planning tonight. She picked the lion king, which he hadn't seen since he had been a little boy. Her good was infectious to him, as he wrapped his arm around her, as she put her head on his shoulder. He was worried that she was tired from being in the hospital the majority of the day, but if she was she made sure to hide it from him. He kissed her forehead, hearing the familiar snap of a picture being taken. He gritted his teeth, knowing the paparazzi had gotten wind of his outing tonight. He ignored them, as they headed into the theater to enjoy the show. He knew, with his status, that he could've gotten private seats, but she had picked it. He didn't want to use it, especially when he wanted to make it about them. As if they were a regular normal couple, when in reality they both came from different worlds of their own. They talked briefly, laughing at someone's ridiculous outfit, before the lights went down and the play began.

By the time it was over, he could see she was tired, the events of today and last night where catching up to her. He kissed her briefly, before taking her hand leading them out of the building, where they met with more flashes of light. A growl of annoyance came from Emily, causing him to smirk, before holding the door open for her and getting in himself. He was thankful that his windows were tinted, just for this reason. Kissing her hand, he saw her yawn.

"Can you stay the night?" She asked him, as she stifled another yawn. He wanted to, but with how wonderful the night had gone, things would happen and he knew she needed her rest.

"Not tonight, baby. I have to see what happened while I was gone."
He told her, his voice holding its own apology. She nodded her head,
as he headed to the underground garage of the apartment building.
He stopped by the elevator shaft, as they kissed passionately for a
few minutes, before he pulled away knowing if one of them hadn't
they be having sex tonight.

"Thank you for tonight. I had a good time." She said to him, kissing
him once more, before opening up her door. She bent down so low,
that he could see a little bit of her panties. Groaning, as he could
feel himself getting hard, he saw the playful smirk on her face as she
leaned in the car, showing a bit of cleavage.

"Good night Emily." He said, squeezing one of her breasts in his
hand, before giving her a look telling her to stop. She sighed, kissing
him once more, before closing the passenger side door. He watched
as she got onto the elevator before driving and back onto the busy
streets of the city.

The moment he got home, he debriefed with his head of security,
before changing into something more comfortable. A pair of sweat
pants, without a shirt on. He found out that Isabelle had planted John
as a spy on them, among other things, which had been a violation in
his book. William had left him a note saying that this was a gold mine,
and the lady herself would be charged in a heartbeat. He rubbed his
face, as he wondered why she was so keen on destroying him, when
he was always several steps ahead. There was no time for a mistake,
as he headed into his office, sitting down in his seat and set to work.

The next morning came, with the sun beaming through the slightly
opened curtains. He stretched out, knowing that he had to deal with
personal issues today. It was something he didn't even want to deal
with, but knew it needed to be done. He had texted Emily telling
her he may be busy for the whole day, considering the big mess that
he had to deal with. He just hoped she would have a good day and
not get too distracted by doing anything foolish. Hell, she had an
entire book collection of first editions she could read from, and he
had a feeling she'd put that to good use, or so he hoped anyways.
Getting up from the bed, he put some casual clothes on, and headed

towards the kitchen where Mrs. Long; his house maid, was cooking breakfast. It smelled delicious to him.

"I hope the guys ate your food last night. I'm sorry I didn't get the chance to." He said to her, sitting at the breakfast bar. He could see the eggs, bacon, hash browns and toast all set out. She always outdid herself in his own opinion.

"It's quite alright, Mr. Bowling. You have some hungry young men, shame how John wanted to hurt you and that gorgeous girl of yours though, sir." She said with a small apologetic smile, as she placed the plate down in front of him, with a glass of orange juice. He sighed, knowing David would be much more careful the next time he hired another staff member.

"Thank you." He simply said to her, before digging into his food. He heard the side door that led out to the security area, open. David came out seeming as he didn't get a good night's sleep, as he sat down next to him opening up a file. Work never stopped and he knew he needed to play catch up with work. He looked through the file, seeing that they all have been blindsided by a few things, important information that shouldn't have been overlooked in the first place. He sighed, wiping off his face with the napkin, before reading the whole entire thing in full. This was definitely going to be a long day, he thought to himself, with a groan. Getting up from the stool, he walked over to the TV seeing as it had something to do with him. Turning up the sound he saw the pictures that had been talked about last night and a video of them briefly kissing outside the Broadway show hall. He smiled, as he could see how happy they looked as they ignored everything around him. It was weird seeing it on screen, it always was to begin with.

"…it may look as if the most eligible bachelor is off the market, Tim." Finished the lady with a look of jealously on her face. The bark of laughter coming from behind him, as David stood next to him.

"It does seem that way, Ruthie. But in other news…" The man continued to babble on, as he turned the volume down. He didn't care to hear any more of it, he just hoped that Emily wouldn't get any shit at work for this, and if she did they'd have to answer to him.

"I'm going for a jog. Then we will somehow manage to get this shit fixed." He told David, who nodded his understanding. He clapped him on the shoulder, before going to his bedroom to put on his running shoes. Checking his phone, there was no response back from Emily. He only hoped, as he put his headphones in his ears, that she was either sleeping or reading, and not getting into some kind of mischief.

The day wore on, he had done an extensive work out session in his work out room, after he had ran a few blocks. The mess that John had created for them, was easily fixed, only because he had left some holes in his quest to ruin him. That had brought a laugh to whole team, especially when he figured out that he slept with his ex to get information out of him. That had puzzled him, as to why he had bothered to break the rules, but it was out of his hands now and in his attorneys. He knew he'd win the case, especially when they had only old statements and facts about him. The piles of emails however, had been another thing he had to tackle, after that whole ordeal. Rubbing his eyes, he just wanted a day of peace and quiet, maybe even a stiff drink. He noticed it was almost dark outside, when he finally got everything done for the day.

"God, I hope this isn't a sign of how this week will be like." Came the voice of David, after knocking on the door to announce his presence. He noticed he was carrying a bottle of what looked to be The Macallan Cask Strength The Highlands Scotch, just by what he could see of the label. It had been awhile since he had tasted some of it, but with the past day and half they both deserved a good strong drink.

"You and me both." He told him, as they clinked glasses after it had been poured. Taking a sip of it, tasting the caramel and vanilla as it went down his throat, before drinking the entire contents of the glass. His phone vibrated, with a text from Emily, smiling he opened it up and saw a bottle of corona and the first edition of; *The Adventures of Tom Sawyer* laying beside it. Chuckling, he showed the picture to David who only shook his head, but had a smile playing on his face at the same time. His phone rang not even a few seconds later.

"I've been in this room allllllllllll day! I finished several books and..."

"Several?! Did you even go to sleep last..."

"Only a few hours, if that. I was just too damn excited to read and..."

"What all have you read?" He asked her, after he had interrupted her yet again. She giggled over the phone, as if it was some big secret. He rolled his eyes, never realizing how happy she would get for books, but even so he had known she was a book lover from the start. He just had given her a reason to read though, after all the majority of those books were first edition and hadn't been cheap either.

"Well let's see.... *The Hobbit, The Catcher in the Rye, Tess of the D'urbervilles.* Though I can't remember where I put Tess at. I got so excited that I re-explored my place and tried a few of the toys in the room." She told him excitedly. As if she had been dying to tell him this news all day. He smirked, as he took another swig of his Scotch, wondering what toys she had tried but wasn't going to ask unless she told him. Essentially he wanted to be surprised for the next time they got intimate with each other.

"Maybe you left it..."

"I want you so bad. I tried the Hitachi Magic Wand and.... you want to see me use it?" She asked, her excitement held a certain anticipation to it. He looked over at David, who didn't need to be told what to do, as he left the room. The door snapping shut behind him.

"Only if you promise me to sleep." He said to her, readjusting himself before getting up from his chair, opening the door and heading towards his bedroom. He picked up his iPad, locked his door and laid down on the bed. He heard her girlish giggle over the phone, before she hung up on him. He FaceTime time her on the iPad, she immediately accepted the call and he laughed when he noticed she was sitting on her bed, a pastry of some sort was next to her on a plate.

"Only if you promise me to sleep." He said to her, readjusting himself before getting up from his chair, opening the door and heading towards his bedroom. He picked up his iPad, locked his door and laid down on the bed.

"I can't make any promises." She told him, as she showed the toy to him on the screen. He readjusted the screen so that he could see her from a better angle. He only done this a few times in the past, but it was only when he was on trips halfway across the world.

"Go ahead." He told her, in a playful time, laughing as she flipped him off. She took her clothes off, even though he noticed she was only wearing a night gown, that had been see through to begin with. His dick felt restrained inside of his pants, as he heard the buzzing of the vibrator come alive on the other end. He watched her place it against her breasts, making them nice and perky, going down in a circular motion before stopping at the head of her pussy. He groaned, knowing she was only doing this to tease him, as he used his hand to stroke his erection. He wanted to close his eyes, imagine that she was here with him, but didn't afraid he would miss something. The light moan escaped from the woman as she placed it against her clit, he noticed that she had readjusted the view to let him see the view better. Oh how he wished he could see this in person. He thought, as he moaned out loud as he continued to pump himself faster. He saw her press it against her swollen lips, as she squirted over the top of it. This was better than porn, it was more intimate and more person than any video he had ever seen on the Internet. He always thought that some of those videos seemed a bit fake, just by how they acted and *pretended* to enjoy what the other person was doing. He knew they got paid for it, at least some of the people on those sites did. Either or it didn't matter right now, seeing as this was one thousand percent better.

He heard her call out his name, breaking him out of his own reverie, as he could tell, just from the way she was moving her hips and fondling one or both her breasts, that she was close. He growled deep, like he had done so many times, in the past month when he wanted her to just let go. She let out a breathy chuckle on the other end, before taking the wand away from her swollen pussy, as she came all over the screen and her sheets. He followed right after, the hunger for her didn't die down though, only made it seem worse than it had before. He fell back onto his bed, bringing the iPad with him. He watched her clean up, before getting under his covers. They talked briefly, before they hung up with each other. After he had cleaned up his mess, he took a brief shower, before getting into be, wishing she was laying down next to him, and not a few miles away. He sighed inwardly, knowing that tomorrow he would see her, and with that thought in mind, he closed his eyes and fell into a deep sleep immediately. His only dreams that night consisted of only her.

CHAPTER 21

A BLARING SOUND MADE HER jump out of the bed, as she pressed the button on the alarm clock to shut it up. It sounded like an annoying car alarm, that made her want to shoot the damn thing to pieces. It had only been a few hours since she had fallen asleep, the book that she had been reading had captured her attention so much that she had lost track of time. Stretching out her limbs, as she pressed the play button on her iPod docking station, to help her get ready for the day. Putting it on high, she took a quick shower, before towel drying her hair, which had been cut the previous day into a bob, with her bangs hanging low in the front. She spiked up the back, as she put on a little mascara, before heading to her closet to see what she should wear for the day. She looked through the many dresses she had, picking out the Red Belted Ponte Dress, putting it on and then choosing a pair of red Darwin heels. She thought she looked amazing, as she put on some red lipstick. Chuckling at the choice of attire, she headed back into her bedroom turning off the iPod dock and headed down the stairs.

She went over to the kitchen, turning on the lights as she fixed herself a bowl of cereal. Nothing worth bragging about but who didn't love Honey Nut Cheerios? She thought to herself, as she finished up her bowl, placed it in the dish washer, before heading out of her place. She turned on the alarm system, that she had managed to figure out after she had set it off the day before, which in turn she didn't bother telling Sean seeing as he had enough on his plate already. Pressing the garage level button, the doors closing shut as she the elevator descended downwards. The doors pinged open a few minutes later, she walked over to her Mustang GT, after giving her two motorcycles a kiss on the seats. She so wanted to ride one of them, which would happen tonight, if she could get mister money bags to come with her. Rolling her eyes, at the name that she had just come up with. Turning on her car, she revved up her engine, and sped out of the garage not even caring about the paparazzi that was staked out at the front entrance waiting for her to come outside.

She got to work, with no worries of heavy traffic, though it was starting to get worse as the morning was starting for everyone. She pulled up into the underground garage, seeing Sean get out of one of his security vehicles. She honked at them, rolled her window down, flipping them off, before parking several spaces down. He was at her drivers door, the moment she turned off her engine, opening the door for her. She hugged his neck, kissing him briefly on the lips, as they clasped hands together. She noticed the extra security around them, as she heard the snapping of pictures being taken in the background.

"Ignore them." He whispered against her ear, which earned him a jab in the rib cage. She hated those people, always thought they were a nuisance to celebrities who just wanted to be like normal people. She made a silent vow, as they stepped into the elevator, that if they ever got into her face she'd punch them; hard. The thought alone made her smirk, but none of them had noticed seeing as they were behind her. She rolled her eyes, knowing they were all thinking she had outdone herself with all the red.

"See you after work." She said, as they arrived at her floor. She gave him a kiss on the cheek, before waving at the rest of the men. Conner following her as she headed towards her office. Turning on the lights, noticing all the paperwork on her desk, as she sat down at her desk. Pressing the button, to turn on her laptop, she began to read the first manuscript on the pile that needed her attention. This was what her job consisted of, and she loved it no matter what happened in her life. This was what she had signed up for.

The morning went by without a hitch, besides the few nosy people who wanted to know how she landed the CEO himself, which she had pointedly ignored. The boss on her floor had even given her grief, but she didn't let it get to her, especially an hour after he had seemed worse for the wear. She hadn't said anything to Sean, but she had known Conner would've done so. He had apologized to her of course, but she threw an eraser at him in retaliation for the whole debacle, causing him to leave the office for the rest of the day. It didn't bother her a bit, as she got up from her chair, walking towards the elevators to see her man, it was lunch time after all. Pressing the up button, she got on after they had opened, as she traveled to the top floor. Getting off, a few minutes later, she noticed that he was shaking hands with an elderly man, before laughing at some joke or another. She cleared her throat, causing all of them to look towards her.

"She's a beauty, Sean. Smoking hot if…"

"William I pay you good money as my lawyer, not to ogle at my girl. Plus I doubt…"

"If you two are done talking about me, I'd like to have a few minutes with my boyfriend. It's nice to meet you though, sir." She said walking over to the both of them, as Sean wrapped his arm around her waist. The older man chuckled, as he kissed her hand in a show of respect.

"William my dear. Sir makes me feel like an old chap." He told her with a wink, as he clapped her man on the shoulder in the process. "She seems like a firecracker. I best be on my way. See you in a few weeks in court." He said, his playful tone gone as it was replaced with a business like tone. She wondered what he meant, but before she could ask the older man anything, he was gone along with four other men behind him. She looked at Sean, waiting for some kind of explanation. He sighed, running his hand through his hair.

"Isabelle is trying to…"

"I get it. I hope the bitch gets what she deserves!" She said through gritted teeth, as she headed into his office, and sitting down in his rolling chair. The door snapped shut a few minutes later, as he turned the seat around.

"You look ravishing today. What is tonight though?" He asked her, curiously as she stood up and wrapped her arms around him. She had missed him the day before, the bed had been way to big for her, but she wasn't going to mention that to him. She didn't want to start sounding clingy now.

"We're going to ride on my motorcycles. I know you..."

"Emily I haven't..."

"It'll be okay. You can ride the Harley, seeing as the Yamaha isn't your type. She'd throw you off in heartbeat." She said as if this wasn't up for argument. He sighed, but didn't say anything back to her as he pulled her back, turning her around looking at her outfit in full. She swayed her hips, which earned her a laugh. Things had changed, between them, since the other night. It was nice to feel wanted by another person, without worry of getting hurt or worse.... used. She sighed inwardly, hoping this wasn't going to end up like the rest of the relationships she had been in, but her father had told her to give him a chance. So that was what she was going to do.

"Will you dance with me?" He asked, breaking the comfortable silence between the two of them.

"Now? There is..."

"Yes now." He said to her, pressing a button on his desk, showing an iPod dock rise out of it. She giggled as she put her head on his chest, as a song started to play. It wasn't loud, nor did it have any words at all, but the musical instruments seemed to have its own words mixed within in. They danced in a slow circle, for several minutes before the slow instrumental song ended, and the familiar intro to Evanescence's song *Bring me to Life* started to play.

> *How can you see into my eyes like open doors?*
> *Leading you down into my core,*
> *Where I've become so numb.*

She had always loved this song, it held such a powerful meaning behind it, it seemed like to her. And as the song continued, she knew that this was her anthem. That she needed to wake up from her own clouded thoughts in the dark and be saved. She looked up at Sean, noticing they had stopped dancing, before kissing hard on the lips. The electricity seemed to ignite like fire between them, as she wanted to connect with his body, feel him inside of her, but knew now wasn't the time either. He pulled away from the mind blowing kiss, their foreheads touching against the other, as they caught their breaths.

"Later, I promise." He whispered, as the song ended and went to another. She turned the iPod off, as she looked him in the eyes. So much was held their, as if the secrets of the world could be told in a matter of seconds, but even she knew he didn't have all the answers for her. It would take baby steps, no matter how small or large they were, to get out of the night that surrounded her thoughts, and into the light to meet him there.

"See you later." She whispered back, not having the heart to talk any louder. She squeezed his hand, before leaving the office. She knew, as she headed towards the elevators and back to her own floor, that it wouldn't be easy. Nothing ever was, but eventually they'd get to the center and find a happy medium.

The rest of the day went by, with tons of paperwork to be read, and notes to make on them, before it was time to go home for the day. She felt content, knowing that she had made it a productive day, as she headed down to the ground level. She had texted Sean earlier just to meet her at her place, before they went out for the ride, as the doors pinged opened several floors from her destination, as more people got on. She didn't really trust herself, if she had met him after getting off of her. Her hormones were still a mess, after the soul searching kiss they had. Walking to her car, after the doors pinged opened, she started up the car and headed towards her apartment building.

Turning the alarm system off, after arriving to her penthouse, she went upstairs to change into some comfortable clothing, before heading back downstairs. Sean was there, dressed casually for once, waiting for her in the small foyer. She giggled, as she was so used to to seeing him in suits and ties, that she had to do a double take. He hugged her, as he pinned a small butterfly to her shirt. It didn't matter why he did it, but she got what he meant without even saying the words. They kissed passionately for a few minutes, before she pulled away and led him over to the equipment. He took the helmet, the pads, and gloves from the wall, as she handed him the keys to her Harley.

"Be gentle with her." She warned him, feeling a bit nervous now that she thought about it. He chuckled before kissing her forehead.

"Don't worry I will be. It's you..."

"I'm an expert. Done this for..."

"Years I'm pretty sure you have. Let's just do this okay?" He said, his voice showing his true emotion. She giggled, as she placed her gloves on her hands, taking the key to the Yamaha off of the shelf. They headed towards the elevator, as she turned the alarm system on, before getting into the cart.

The ride down to the garage floor, seemed to take forever, but really only took a few minutes as the doors opened wide and they headed to the two shining black bikes that seemed to shine brighter than ever. She smirked, as she rubbed the side of her bike, before kissing the seat. She hadn't done that till she had almost wrecked it a month back. Hopping onto the bike, she started the engine, as she watched him doing the same thing. She had her doubts about him, but wasn't going to mention that right now over the loud engines, as she revved her engine up. She signaled to him to go ahead, and as they peeled out of the garage, the flashing of lights followed suit after them.

After a few minutes though, when they finally got out of the main city, she led the way down the highway. The wind could be felt on her back, as her shirt rose up with the wind. The feeling of absolute freedom came to her, as she completely forgot about anything else that had happened recently, and drove down the open road, with Sean right beside her.

Printed in the United States
By Bookmasters